ALEX NEPTUNE

DRAGON THIEF

"THERE'S NO SUCH THING
AS A SEA MONSTER,"
ALEX SAID FIRMLY.

(SPOILER: HE WAS WRONG.)

For Teddy,

Hard-earned, well-deserved, so loved.

First published in the UK in 2022 by Usborne Publishing Ltd., Usborne House, 83-85 Saffron Hill, London EC1N 8RT, England. usborne.com

Usborne Verlag, Usborne Publishing Ltd., Prüfeninger Str. 20, 93049 Regensburg, Deutschland VK Nr. 17560

A CIP catalogue record for this book is available from the British Library.

ISBN 9781474999236   7445/1   JFMAM JASOND/22

Printed and bound in Great Britain by CPI Group (UK) Ltd, Croydon, CR0 4YY.

MIX
Paper from
responsible sources
FSC® C171272

ALEX NEPTUNE
DRAGON THIEF

DAVID OWEN

USBORNE

CONTENTS

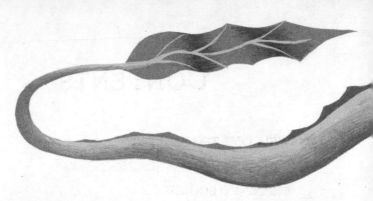

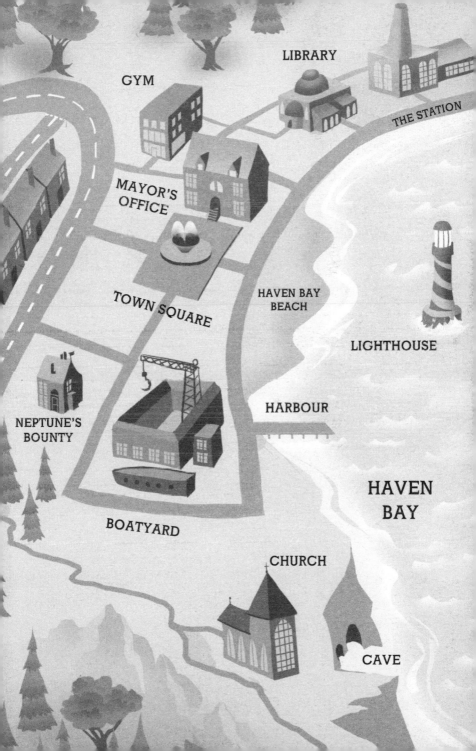

CHAPTER ONE

For as long as Alex Neptune could remember, the sea had been trying to kill him.

The very first time he dipped a toe into the ocean, a rogue wave had crashed over his head and swept him off his feet. Ever since, a gentle paddle would summon the tide foaming high to drag him out of his depth, a timid swim inviting seaweed to wrap fast around his legs and haul him under. His mere presence could provoke vicious currents and monstrous swells from the calmest seas.

Everybody told Alex it was just bad luck. Only he knew the truth.

The ocean wanted him dead.

The cause of this maritime grudge remained a mystery,

so his best chance of surviving it was to stay away from the water altogether.

Which was a problem when he had lived his entire life in the seaside town of Haven Bay.

"I got my underwear wet."

Zoey Wu, his best friend, squelched up the beach from the waterline. Although her clothes were dripping wet, the sea had failed to wash away the black grease smeared across her cheeks or the sawdust shavings stuck in her straight black fringe. She lived at the local boatyard with her dad, who handled repairs and sold spare parts to fund his dream of becoming an artist, creating bizarre sculptures from scrap metal in his spare time. Zoey spent the summer holidays pretending to help, while secretly stealing bits and bobs to transform into what she claimed were brilliant inventions. Alex had lost count of the number of times she had accidentally burned off her eyebrows.

"Can you *please* hurry up?" Alex pressed his back against the sea wall, as far away from the lapping tide as he could get.

"You shouldn't hate the ocean so much," Zoey said. "It hasn't tried to murder you in ages."

Alex didn't *hate* the ocean. The repeated assassination attempts – as well as Grandpa expressly forbidding him from going anywhere near it – had simply left him terrified of it. Sometimes he was sure the ocean actually taunted him. Waves pealing against shore, wind whistling over rocks, seagulls cackling in wheeling circles – it all felt as if the water was beckoning him into its clutches so it could finish him off for good.

He shivered and turned away towards town. Haven Bay was an old fishing village built on a hill that lifted steeply from the ocean. It rose in layers: first, the wide sea wall bounded the beach, topped by the wooden-framed shops and cobbles of the high street, with the old harbour and the boatyard at one side of the bay.

The next layer up the hill was multicoloured houses, faded to pastel shades by countless summers, tottering against each other like a pirate's crooked teeth. Above those was a thick strip of trees and bushes rising steeply up until the hill flattened at its highest point.

There, Alex could just see the domed glass structure housing the aquarium. The unlikely location had been selected a century before by an eccentric mayor who believed visitors would enjoy the panoramic sea view. Unfortunately, this made the aquarium extravagantly expensive to operate and it had finally closed down a few years ago. Now the empty tanks inside the grand glass walls had been left to rot.

"Let's find out what's *really* in the water." Zoey had

collected a jam jar of seawater. It had taken months of begging before her dad had agreed to buy her a chemistry set so they could perform some tests. Now she busied herself wedging test tubes into the sand and filling them up.

While she squeezed droplets into the tubes, Alex gazed out across the bay. The shifting waves smouldered under the broad disc of the setting sun. An unruly formation of seabirds was making its raucous return to roosts in the nearby cliffs.

It would have been beautiful, were it not for the litter that smothered the water. Carrier bags and plastic bottles, tins and crisp packets, yoghurt pots and cotton buds formed floating bands of filth. Oil glistened on the surface of the waves. The lapping water left a shifting black tideline of gunk along the beach.

Barely a year had passed since Mayor Humbertus Parch took control of Haven Bay and approved construction of a mysterious facility known as the Station. The grey concrete building perched on the water's edge like an unsightly barnacle. Apart from the arrival or departure of the occasional boat, nobody was ever seen going in or out. Security guards in black uniforms stood watch outside every hour of the day.

The mayor claimed the Station monitored water quality. But shortly after it was built the water turned foul and tourists stopped showing up. It couldn't be a coincidence. In the pub, cafe and chip shop, locals grumbled their suspicions about the Station. But whenever anybody tried to investigate, key documents would conveniently disappear and professional water-testing teams would find their equipment sabotaged overnight.

Alex and Zoey hoped that Mayor Parch wouldn't notice two kids with a chemistry set. If they could prove the Station was to blame, Alex was sure the town would rise up and fight to get it shut down.

"What the heck?" said Zoey, snatching his attention.

The water inside the test tubes had turned a series of bright colours: orange, purple and a particularly sickly green.

"All of those are normal. This is the only one I don't understand." Zoey picked up the last tube in the row. The water inside had turned sludgy and grey like blended mussels. "There's a substance in the water I don't recognize."

"Could *that* be why it's so filthy?" asked Alex. "There can't be anything living out there by now. Nobody can even go swimming any more."

"At least that means they can't get eaten by sharks," said Zoey.

"We don't have sharks here," replied Alex. Over the years he had researched every sea creature in the world capable of killing him. He figured there was no harm in being prepared. "And I've already told you, they hardly ever attack people."

"That's what the sharks want you to think," Zoey countered. "People go out there all the time, right, so it must be safe. And then *snap!* They get chomped the heck in half."

Alex shuddered. "There are way more dangerous things living in the ocean."

"Like the Water Dragon?"

Like most old seaside towns, Haven Bay was rife with stories and legends handed down over centuries. Alex knew all about them from the books his family sold in their souvenir shop. And every single local legend was tied to a mythical sea monster called the Water Dragon that had supposedly created the bay.

The story went that hundreds of years ago the people who lived along this shore forged a connection with a dragon that ruled over the waves. It gave them powers, allowing them to breathe underwater, live unnaturally long lives and communicate with the sea creatures they lived alongside.

All of that changed when the people betrayed the Water Dragon. In its fury, the dragon took an enormous bite out of the coast, destroying their civilization and forming the bay.

It would be a century before the dragon returned to Haven Bay.

Alex had always loved the stories, but now he was older he suspected they had been invented by bored fishermen and their hazy details exaggerated as they were handed down through the generations.

"There's no such thing as sea monsters," he said firmly.

Which was exactly when they heard a terrible gargle and turned to find a monster with an octopus for a head staggering along the beach towards them.

CHAPTER TWO

NO SUCH THING AS
SEA MONSTERS

Before Alex could move, Zoey had snatched up her shoes
to wield as weapons.

"Sea monster!" she bellowed.

The shoes smacked against the monster's side and sent
it rolling dramatically onto the sand.

"Ow!" it cried. "A mortal wound! The end of a short but
beautiful life!"

Alex reached out to stop the footwear onslaught. "I
recognize that voice."

Zoey ignored him and lifted the shoes again. "Die, vile
fiend from the depths!"

The monster's distinctly human hand reached up to
peel away the octopus firmly attached to its face. Eight

suckered limbs popped stubbornly from the skin beneath as it flailed to cling on.

Anil Chatterjee grinned at them from underneath, face covered in round sucker marks. "It's not a sea monster, it's me!"

Grudgingly, Zoey lowered her weapons. "Yeah, I knew that already."

Alex rushed forwards to peer closer. "Where did you get *that*?"

The octopus had now wrapped itself in a tight embrace around the boy's elbow. Its bulbous head was a deep, splotchy blue and orb-like eyes with narrow pupils seemed to squint at them all with shrewd suspicion. Its body would fit in the palm of his hand, but its long limbs made it seem much larger.

"Stay away from its tentacles, they'll sting you!" shrieked Zoey while simultaneously pushing for a closer look.

"They're not tentacles, they're *arms*. And they can't sting you." Alex peered at the octopus. "I didn't think anything was living out there any more. Where did you find it?"

"In one of the tunnels. I think it was lost. It seemed keen to hitch a ride." Anil gave the octopus a tentative poke. "I was coming here to bring it to you. I heard you know all about this stuff?"

Anil's family had moved into town a few months ago after his parents took jobs as doctors at the local hospital. The boy had immediately tried to make friends with Alex and Zoey, sitting nearby at school and attempting to impress them with jokes and stories. Alex didn't mind, but the new arrival had brought out a fiercely protective streak in Zoey, whose cold shoulder made it clear Anil should stay away. Now he seemed to spend all his free time exploring every nook and cranny of Haven Bay.

"You shouldn't be in those tunnels!" warned Zoey. "Don't blame me when you drown!"

Anil grinned again. "No need to worry about me. I used to go to the swimming pool with my cousins every weekend. I can hold my breath for *ages*. Like, whole minutes. Hours, probably!"

"And yet he never stops talking," she muttered.

Every child who grew up in Haven Bay was taught about the dragon tunnels. Although the nearby cliffs appeared imposingly sheer, at their base began a honeycomb of narrow shafts and serpentine burrows. The stories insisted the Water Dragon had carved them out and stuffed them with riches beyond imagining. Nowadays they were considered little more than deathtraps. At low tide you could easily walk along the beach and climb into the caves and passages. But the ocean could rush back in with wicked quickness to trap anybody still inside. Alex suffered a recurring nightmare where he was trapped in the darkness of a tapering tunnel as the water rose mercilessly around his neck...

The stories only encouraged Anil to ignore the dangers and stubbornly scour the cliff passages for lost treasure. The most he had discovered so far was a few glass bottles and a set of rotten wooden teeth.

Anil lifted the octopus to give Alex a closer look. The octopus unfurled its arms, crawled swiftly along Anil's wrist, and plopped onto Alex's shoulder. He froze, half-expecting the creature to attempt to strangle him.

"It's like a living bogey," Zoey declared. "I think I love it."

Anil opened his mouth to speak, just as a pink iced bun, missing a single crescent-shaped bite, dropped from the sky and bounced off his head. Moments later a plump seagull landed, flapping, on his shoulder. A band of grey feathers was sketched across its wings.

"Pinch!" Anil shouted at the bird. "I told you to stop stealing food from people!"

The gull simply tilted his head and nipped affectionately at Anil's hair.

Anil had found Pinch in the school playground, struggling with an injured wing. Seeking medical advice from his parents, Anil had lovingly nursed him back to health. The bird had refused to leave him alone ever since, choosing to repay his saviour by snatching snacks from unsuspecting townspeople and offering them as unwanted gifts.

"A thieving seagull is not the kind of friend my parents want me to make," Anil said. He retrieved the hijacked bun, icing now crunchy with sand. "Anybody want some?"

Pinch thrashed his wings and lifted himself into the sky to join the straggling birds still returning from sea. Alex craned his neck to watch as the sun slipped closer to the horizon.

"That's weird," he said.

The birds weren't settling on the cliffs. Usually the rocky face was so restless with beaks and feathers that it appeared alive. Tonight, a mass of seabirds had bypassed the cliff to gather over the top of the town, above the old aquarium house, wheeling and shifting in chaotic formation.

"I've never seen them do that before," said Alex.

Zoey and Anil were too busy arguing over how much seawater you'd have to drink before you'd vomit to pay any attention. The gathering grew larger by the second as more birds streamed to join from every direction, an ominous shadow see-sawing across the darkening sky. The cacophony of their cries seemed to bounce off the glass dome of the aquarium like a siren, making Alex shiver.

When he was younger, Alex had forced himself to visit the aquarium to face his fears. There had been a thrill to cautiously watching the glamorous fish and heavily armoured lobsters, shimmying eels and hustling turtles. He was fascinated by creatures that could survive three miles under the waves, liquefy their bodies to escape being eaten, glow and shimmer with alien light. The ocean was a harsh environment for them too, but unlike him they had found a way to withstand it.

Now, long after the aquarium had closed, it had begun to drown his dreams. For the last two nights he had dreamed he was locked inside the glass structure. Ghosts of the animals that had lived there were trapped inside their old tanks. They banged against the glass, louder and louder, begging to be released, until Alex fell out of bed and jerked awake.

He should have told Zoey about the nightmares, but it was bad enough being so scared of the sea when his best friend didn't seem to be scared of *anything*.

And now the birds circled over the domed glass roof of the aquarium as if they were being drawn to it.

"Something is wrong," said Alex, unsure why the words sprang unbidden to his lips but feeling their truth in his gut. In response, the octopus cradled itself in the crook of his elbow. It was almost cute, gazing up at him with quizzical eyes. "You *definitely* shouldn't be here."

"You should take it home and make sure it's okay," said Zoey.

The octopus agreed by tightening its grip on his arm. Apparently Alex didn't have much choice.

CHAPTER THREE

NEPTUNE'S BOUNTY

When the aquarium closed down, Alex's dad had decided to rehome some of the smaller creatures in the hope it would help Alex overcome his fear of the ocean. Plus they made for colourful displays around the shop.

The plan was scuppered when a tank burst in the middle of the night. Alex had been too scared to help with the rescue effort, and for weeks afterwards they were surprised by shrimp in the sink, crabs in the kettle, and a crayfish that found its way into the toilet to give Dad a startling nip from underneath.

So he probably wouldn't be too thrilled to lay eyes on the octopus Alex carried home in a bright plastic bucket full of seawater.

Neptune's Bounty – the tourist shop Alex's family owned and that he lived above with his dad, grandad and sister – was closed for the night. Their ice cream van – which Grandpa ran, mainly to get the grumpy old man away from the shop as much as possible – was parked outside. While Alex fumbled for his key at the front door, the octopus clambered out of the bucket and onto his shoulder.

"You're not a parrot!" Alex told it. Though now he looked, the elegant swoop of its body and the backwards curve of its egg-shaped head – like a crown of plumage – lent it an oddly bird-like profile.

The shop was themed around the most famous part of the Water Dragon legend. A century after taking a bite out of the coast and creating the bay, the dragon had returned, chased there by a notorious pirate called Captain Brineblood. The pirate was obsessed with capturing the creature and wielding its power for evil deeds. Brineblood cornered the Water Dragon in the bay and deployed a blockade of ships to trap it there.

At the next full moon, a storm whipped up that was so powerful it could only have been summoned by the dragon. The raging waves dashed Brineblood's ship to pieces and scattered the others. The captain was swallowed up whole by the Water Dragon before it once again swam free.

Every year since, under the August full moon, the legend

told that Brineblood's hollow-eyed ghost dragged itself from the ocean to roam the streets of Haven Bay in search of fresh crewmen to sail his drowned ship.

The story was so popular that tourists flocked to the town every summer for the famous Water Dragon ceremony. Everybody put up a grotesque Brineblood scarecrow outside their homes to scare the evil pirate wraith away. And when the full moon rose, a model Water Dragon was paraded through the streets and released into the ocean to escape.

It was only three days until the full moon. So alongside the irregular shadows of buckets and spades, rubber rings and snorkels hanging from hooks along the wall, the shop boasted a dragon crafted from braids of brightly coloured paper trailing around the ceiling.

Alex slipped behind the counter to retrieve an old glass tank. Next, carefully balancing everything, he tiptoed to the door that led to the area behind the shop they called home. If he could just make it upstairs without Dad or Grandpa spotting him...

A skeleton confronted him on the other side of the door. Alex yelped and nearly dropped the tank. Then he realized it was the unfinished Brineblood scarecrow Dad and Mr Wu were making together. A metal skull was propped on a broom-handle spine and straw poked from the bottom of a tattered jacket where the legs should have been.

Before Alex could grab the octopus from his shoulder, Dad poked his head around the kitchen door. Alex braced for the first shout of outrage.

"Dinner in ten minutes, love." Dad winked, before ducking back into the kitchen.

Alex glanced at his shoulder.

The octopus was gone.

Frantically he scanned the empty tank and peered down into the bucket of seawater. It was nowhere to be seen.

The octopus's head appeared out of thin air in front of him. Alex yelled in surprise. Slowly, eight blue arms shimmered into existence, clinging firmly to the front of his black T-shirt.

"Camouflage," Alex whispered. The octopus had shifted the colour of its skin to match the shirt so it wouldn't be seen.

He hurried upstairs and shut himself inside his bedroom. The tank already had a carpet of gravel and pebbles, and Alex worked quickly to stack some of the small rocks to form a shelter. Then he dumped the seawater inside and bent his shoulder to the lip of the tank.

The octopus extended an inquisitive arm to test the water, like a reluctant bather dipping their toe into a rock pool, before it shifted itself forwards and plopped into the tank. It sank to the bottom and immediately set about redecorating the tank to its liking. Alex closed the tank lid and marvelled at the dexterity of the octopus's arms, organizing stones like a master geologist. Every arm was covered in suckers, meaning it must be female.

He opened his laptop and typed a description of the octopus into a search engine.

After a few minutes of examining different images he identified her. "You're a big blue octopus," he told her. "*Octopus cyanea*. You come from Hawaii. Or the east coast of Africa!" He pressed his nose against the cool glass side of the tank. "So what are you doing here?"

The octopus broke off from her construction work and propelled herself closer to the glass. Her skin flickered like a sheet of electric lights. Blue shimmered to white. More colours began to strobe across the fleshy globe of the octopus's head: ocean green, summery yellow, floral purple.

"That's incredible," Alex breathed, fogging the glass. No wonder sailors used to believe the ocean was brimming with monsters. "I'm going to call you Kraken."

The colours blinked again, this time the octopus's whole body flaring a feverish red like a warning signal.

"If you don't like the name, I can call you something else!" Alex said in surprise.

The red only blazed more intensely. Kraken gave a coordinated flick of her arms and launched herself like a torpedo at the lid of the tank. The plastic top jolted alarmingly but held firm. The octopus hit it again, before changing tactics to probe the side of the tank closest to the bedroom window. One arm peeled away from the others to point outside. Alex's mouth dropped open in disbelief. Octopuses couldn't *point*. But Kraken seemed particularly insistent, so Alex turned to look.

Night had almost fallen. A loose spiral of street lights and dimly illuminated houses marked out the rise of the hill above them. The darkness usually made the top of the hill, where the old aquarium stood, a black void near indistinguishable from the sky.

Tonight, an eerie green light glowed there.

The glow emanated from exactly where the seabirds had been circling less than an hour before. It seemed to call to Alex, *insist* he come closer, luring him like a moth to a light bulb.

Suddenly Alex remembered being woken up after midnight two nights ago by a truck rumbling past outside. He had made it to the window just in time to see it trundling towards the aquarium. The bad dreams had started that same night, as soon as he went back to bed, disturbing his sleep so badly he had forgotten about the truck until now.

He turned back to the octopus. "You want to go there?"

Kraken extended another arm as if to emphasize her point.

"No way," said Alex, fighting the pull of the glow. "I am *not* going to the spooky abandoned aquarium in the dark."

Before there was any chance to argue further – not that he was sure he *could* truly argue with an octopus – Dad called him for dinner. Alex tore his gaze away from the eerie green light and hurried downstairs.

There was no room in the kitchen for a table so they always ate at the shop's counter, which meant dinner couldn't happen until the shop was closed. Alex sank into a fold-out camping chair, Chonkers the cat – named for her particularly generous proportions – winding around his legs. Grandpa sat opposite, eyeing the unappetizing food with a deep-lined frown. Somehow there was already tomato ketchup smeared on his bald head.

Alex noticed there was only one more chair at the counter. "How come Bridget always gets to skip dinner?"

"Your sister is on her special weightlifting diet," said Dad, dishing out steaming heaps of mashed potato.

"Have you tried usin' the bathroom after her since she's been on this diet?" asked Grandpa, waving a hand in front of his nose.

"We have to respect Bridget's goals no matter how pungent the side effects."

"Mind you, nothin' stinks worse than the water out there in the bay," Grandpa grumbled. "What tourist wants to visit a beach covered in litter and smellin' like a latrine? Your grandma would be scullin' in her grave if she were here to see it."

Five years had passed since Grandma died. Although she'd always worked hard to keep the beaches clean, she had refused to so much as dip a toe into the sea. And after the first time the water attacked Alex, she and Grandpa had forbidden him from going near it too. The ocean was dangerous, Grandma told him. One of his strongest memories of her was standing together on the sea wall, watching others swim and play in the waves, while she held his hand so tightly he was sure he could still feel her grip now.

"The Station pollutes the bay—" said Alex.

Dad interrupted through a mouthful of potato. "Nothing we've tried has allowed us to prove that."

"But where does all the litter come from?"

"Everythin' what's been done to damage this place is messin' with the balance of nature," Grandpa grunted. "Who knows what nature might do to us in return?"

Alex brightened. "Well, if there are no tourists coming

any time soon, maybe I can be let off my shift tomorrow morning..."

Dad shook his head fiercely. "Just because it's the summer holiday doesn't mean you can spend all day running wild. If it's quiet, you can help me and Mr Wu finish off our Brineblood scarecrow! It's going to be *extra* creepy this year!"

Alex glanced into the hallway where the scarecrow was still perched. A much more frightening sight made him choke on his dinner. Kraken the octopus was crawling along the carpet towards the shop.

"No!" he shouted.

Dad and Grandpa paused with forks halfway to their mouths.

"Uh, no *way* can anybody make a better scarecrow than you!" He shot to his feet and ran for the hallway. *"Can-I-be-excused-thank-you-it-was-delicious!"*

Alex scooped up the octopus as he ran and bundled through to the kitchen.

"You *really* want to go to the aquarium. Is that why you travelled all the way from Africa?"

Kraken stretched out an arm to grab Alex's chin and nod his head up and down like a puppet.

It seemed the aquarium was his best chance of finding any answers to all the strange things that had happened in the last two days. "All right, *fine*."

Alex took a plastic takeaway box from the cupboard – being boneless meant Kraken could easily squeeze inside – and hurried out of the back door before anybody could see him.

He didn't make it past the garage before the door slid up and open. K-pop music blared out onto the driveway.

"Where do you think *you're* running off to at this time of night?"

Bridget Neptune gripped an oversized dumb-bell in one hand, the other swiping beads of sweat from her forehead. A bright pink vest strained over her hulking shoulders. Alex couldn't quite remember when his big sister had become his *BIG* sister. The weight training had been inspired by her embarrassing failure to open a stubborn ketchup bottle in the school canteen. Nobody expected her enthusiasm to last longer than a week. So it was quite a shock when her biceps began tearing through the sleeves of her T-shirts and she had thoroughly trounced the personal bests of every single boy in the local gym.

Alex was fairly sure his sister could snap him in half with her bare hands. These days, he tried to stay on her good side.

There was just enough time to hide the octopus behind

his back. "Hi, Bridget! Are you, uh, totally blasting those gains to the max?" he asked sweetly.

"Oh my *gosh*, don't even ask me that." Bridget studied the immaculate nail varnish on her free hand. "My delts are, like, totally shredded, and I can't even boost the poundage for a proper pump."

Alex nodded along politely. As far as he was concerned a pump was something you put in a fish tank.

Bridget flexed her arm. It swelled like a prize-winning pufferfish.

"I swear there's, like, *no way* Coach Barge won't select me for the team this year."

Last year the weightlifting team had refused to let her join. Although the coach didn't say so, Bridget was convinced it was because she was a girl. Try-outs for next year were in a couple of days. She had been working overtime to make sure she would beat all the boys and they couldn't reject her again.

Bridget tossed a flawlessly highlighted strand of hair over her shoulder. "Watch out for Brineblood if you're going for a walk."

"I don't believe in any of that."

She shrugged. "Suit yourself. He's probably stalking the streets right now waiting to peel your skin off. Don't come crying to me when he turns your scalp into a fashionable hat. Actually, forget it. No part of you could *ever* be fashionable." She returned to her weights, slamming the garage door closed behind her.

Kraken smouldered red again and pushed impatiently against the side of the plastic box. Alex wasn't going to be scared by an old story of a ghostly pirate. Instead, he surrendered to the nagging pull of the green glow and let it lead him towards the top of the hill.

CHAPTER FOUR

WONDERS OF THE DEEP SEA (NOW CLOSED)

Alex immediately felt scared by the old story of a ghostly pirate.

"It's just a stupid scary folk tale," he told himself as he hurried up the hill.

The road doubled back and forth across the face of the hill, rising higher all the time. Brineblood scarecrows were skewered on wooden posts outside every house. Alex tried to keep his eyes away from the scrawled faces and crooked limbs. Light from the old rock lighthouse stationed at the mouth of the bay flashed across the water intermittently, casting fleetingly eerie shadows throughout the town.

Halfway up the hill, Alex spotted a white light bobbing

fitfully towards him. He shielded his eyes to recognize Mrs Bilge shuffling along the pavement, a head torch strapped over her white hair. Behind her waddled her old dog Cannonball, surely named for his round, sagging belly that swept the ground as he walked.

The old lady swivelled her head to aim the light at the plastic box tucked under Alex's arm. "What have you got there?"

"I'm just, um…taking my octopus for a walk." Alex had never been brilliant at coming up with excuses. Kraken waved an arm in greeting.

Mrs Bilge adjusted her glasses, squinted at Kraken balled inside the tub, and gave an approving nod. "It's important to get them exercise. I have to keep my Cannonball here in tip-top shape!"

The old dog wheezed and rolled onto his side like a beached seal. Mrs Bilge tugged sharply at the lead, dragging Cannonball away in her wake.

At the top of the hill, the winding road straightened onto a long driveway lined with overgrown trees and black iron lamp posts, their light long since faded. Alex had to feel his way cautiously through the darkness to reach the tall gate of the old aquarium, rusted and hanging open.

HAVEN BAY AQUARIUM read a sign above the gate. *HOME TO THE WONDERS OF THE DEEP SEA!*

The aquarium had been built over a hundred years ago; an imposing house of iron and glass set against the sky. The curved roof rose into a grand domed top. It must have sparkled like a jewel once. Now the panes of glass that forged its walls and roof were cracked and spattered with bird droppings. A *CLOSED* sign hung crookedly on the entrance doors. Underneath it in red paint somebody had scrawled *FOR EVER*.

Kraken grew more agitated now they had reached the aquarium. She climbed up to perch on the rim of the plastic box. The tug of the green glow was so much stronger here. Alex pushed the glass doors but a heavy padlock held them closed.

"We're not getting in this way."

Nearby, part of the glass wall had long ago cracked and fallen away, leaving a gap just wide enough for him to carefully squeeze inside.

The old display tanks stood like portals to drowned worlds where strange and fearsome creatures once reigned. The wide entrance hall narrowed like a funnel into the boulevard of glass tanks that formed the central path of the aquarium – Oceanic Avenue. Most of the tanks still brimmed with murky water, brown gunk drifting like autumn leaves falling in slow motion. Enough light from the nearly full moon shone through the glass ceiling high above to pick out sunken ornaments – diving bells, shipwrecks, stone sea serpents – bearded with thick skins of algae.

The glow intensified as Alex let it pull him along the faded mosaic path between the tanks and along the length of the aquarium. The inhabitants were long gone, but Alex couldn't shake the feeling that he was being watched, as if the ghosts from his dreams were real.

To one side, a crudely painted sign invited visitors to enter *BRINEBLOOD'S GHOST SHIP*. Inside, a sharp-toothed animatronic dragon used to burst from the waves and gobble up a dummy dressed as a pirate. Now the entrance was shuttered and sealed.

Kraken tugged on the edge of the box to urge them onwards. At its furthest end, Oceanic Avenue led to a soaring archway fitted with tall, baroque double doors. As he approached, one side creaked haltingly open. Green light spilled out. A series of rapid *click-click-clicks* skittered ahead of him, punctuated by short, sharp squeaks. Alex felt his legs lock with fear. Still, the light seemed to beckon him. He took a breath of stale air and forced himself to step through the archway.

The back of the park had housed the main attraction: the dolphin tank. A hexagonal wall of glass long and sheer, twice his height. Although Alex knew now that the tank had always been a cruel prison for animals as energetic and free as dolphins, their lithe and limber antics had never failed to delight him as a child.

A dense jacket of algae and impenetrably cloudy water disguised the source of the green glow inside the tank. Still, it cast enough light to pick out four scampering shapes on the path. Alex yelped in surprise.

Four sea otters froze and peered up at him warily. Each carried a fish in their jaws. Clearly his arrival had interrupted their work, though what exactly that was remained unclear.

"Um, sorry?" he said.

The otters tilted their heads in consideration. Button noses sniffed, sprays of whiskers waggling. Kraken clambered onto Alex's shoulder and shifted her colour to mirror the soft green shining from the tank.

Apparently this was signal enough for the otters to resume their business. One by one they dropped their catch at the base of the tank. The largest of them then huddled low so that another could clamber onto its back. The third repeated the trick before the smallest otter carefully ascended the teetering stack to perch at the top.

Next, the fish were passed up mouth-to-mouth, deftly tossed and caught, for the otter at the pinnacle to sling over the top of the tank and into the water.

A realization shuddered through Alex. "They're feeding something."

Kraken climbed up onto his head and yanked painfully at his hair, like a cowboy taming a wild horse. Alex dutifully inched closer to the glowing water.

A sudden whisper almost knocked him over with fright. He glanced around in panic but there was nobody else there. Yet a voice nagged at him, spoken in waves breaking and seabed shifting. The same voice the ocean used to taunt him. It was coming from inside the tank. Alex prepared to run. Except...the voice was filled with sadness. Defeat. Whatever it belonged to was *trapped* there. And it was asking him for... Every time Alex almost caught the word it was washed out of his reach.

Taking a breath to steady himself, Alex lifted a hand and pressed it against the cool glass of the tank. The glow inside intensified, responding to his touch. It cut through the floating filth like a lighthouse beam, breaking apart the algae on the inside of the tank. The glass grew clear in a perfect imprint of his hand.

Every beat of Alex's heart felt like a depth charge detonating. Whatever was inside the tank was asking him to look. He lowered his eyes to the cleared portal. The water was still grubby, but the green radiance revealed a little of what lay inside.

A coiled, grey shape, lying still. A sunken log, perhaps, or a piece of broken machinery left to rust.

Until it moved.

An eye opened on the other side of the glass. Its milky pupil caught him in its ravenous gaze.

Alex cried out and staggered away from the tank, bowling over the tower of otters. The animals chattered indignantly as they scattered apart.

"Hey!"

The shout echoed from the other side of the archway, bouncing around the glass walls. Alex whirled around to see torchlight wavering closer.

The green glow inside the dolphin tank vanished like a snuffed candle, plunging him into darkness. The otters rushed away past his ankles. A tug at his hair from Kraken shocked Alex to his senses. He turned to run just as the beam of a torch picked him out.

"Who's there?" demanded its owner.

The archway was blocked. Alex was trapped. There was no choice but to surrender.

Still perched on top of his head, Kraken reared up tall like a spitting cat and let fly a jet of water towards the torchlight. A startled cry was followed by the light clattering to the ground.

Now Alex didn't waste any time. He barrelled through the archway, ran back along the promenade of barren tanks, and escaped through the gap in the wall.

CHAPTER FIVE

MAYOR OF MONSTERS

Sparks showered from the scrap metal sword as Mr Wu welded it into the scarecrow's hand.

"Perfect!" said Dad, watching from the shelter of the shop doorway. "It looks just like him."

Alex studied a postcard of Brineblood – the only known portrait of the evil pirate. Greasy hair spilled from beneath a battered, wide-brimmed hat, his sneer revealing a chequerboard of missing teeth. One foot was propped on a cannon, a wickedly sharp harpoon held in a grubby hand. The caption read:

Captain Brineblood
He crushed these seas under heel.

Zoey's mum was visiting family in China for the summer, so Mr Wu had decided to combine his artistic skills with Alex's dad's unskilled enthusiasm to enter the scarecrow competition together. Their entry was a skeleton elegantly forged from buckled boat propellers, dressed in old clothes from Dad's wardrobe stuffed with straw.

"This is my year!" said Dad. "It's time to break that decade-long losing streak!"

Alex yawned and rubbed his eyes. Dreams of the aquarium park – of an eye opening in murky water, an abysmal black form calling out in pain – had repeatedly tipped him overboard from sleep throughout the night.

"So it's a cyborg pirate who found all his clothes in a bag on the side of the road," said Zoey, who had trailed along with her dad.

Mr Wu took off his protective welding mask to reveal a face stained with grease just like his daughter's. "You have no appreciation of art."

Zoey scoffed. "I just prefer making things that are actually useful."

"Art *is* useful. If you applied more artistry to your inventions, maybe they wouldn't be quite so likely to explode."

Her face screwed up into a frown. "Can we please go now?" she said to Alex.

Most mornings of their summer holiday had been spent combing the rubbish freshly washed up on the beach for junk Zoey needed for her latest invention, and she was keen to hunt for the final required item.

Dad shook his head. "Alex has to work in the shop."

"Can't I go for a few hours?" Alex begged. "There hasn't been a single customer since we opened."

Sadly, he was right. They had opened promptly two hours ago, but nobody had so much as glanced in the window.

"All right, fine." Dad looked between them gravely. "Just the rest of the morning! Make sure you're back by lunchtime."

"And be careful what you go rummaging through!" added Mr Wu.

Alex and Zoey left their fathers to put up the scarecrow outside the shop and hurried to the beach.

The black tide had washed carrier bags, shreds of netting, plastic bottles and ready-meal containers high up the sand. A chemical smell edged the morning air. Together they picked doggedly through the litter for anything Zoey could use.

"It smells like dirt under a big toenail," she said, pinching a sodden sponge between the fingers of her bright yellow rubber gloves. Underneath was a tangle of wires braided with seaweed. Zoey seized it triumphantly. "Yes! This is exactly what I need!"

Although Zoey's inventions were built with good intentions, they had a habit of going spectacularly wrong with very little warning. There had been the self-guiding life raft that would only guide itself towards rocks, before exploding. Oh, and the seawater purifier that instead of producing drinkable water turned it into a corrosive paste that smelled like rotten fish guts. And then exploded. In fact, Alex struggled to think of any of her inventions that *hadn't* exploded.

"Don't look at me like that!" she said. "Right now my drone only catches fire a little bit when it turns left."

A flying drone would allow them to spy on the Station and find out what was really going on in there. Zoey had been trying to perfect it since the start of the holidays.

She kicked grumpily at a block of driftwood, grumbling under her breath.

"Are you okay?" asked Alex.

"My dad thinks art is more important than technology. I want to show him that what I do *is* important. But I can't do that if my inventions don't work." Zoey gazed around the beach. "Technology doesn't have to just hurt the environment. I want to use it to help too. When we save the bay, he'll finally see."

"You *are* helping. Just don't rush it." Too often her enthusiasm outstripped her patience. "It's going to be amazing."

Zoey grinned. "It'll blow my dad's artsy-fartsy socks off."

Alex reached down to turn over a butter tub. A crab sheltering underneath brandished its claws at him in protest.

"I saw something weird last night," he said.

"Bridget oiling up her muscles again?"

Alex shuddered at the memory. "Not that. I went up to the old aquarium."

Now he had her attention. She stuffed the wiring into her pocket and grabbed his arm. "It's haunted, isn't it? I knew it! I *told* you I heard the ghostly squeals of dead dolphins late at night."

"It wasn't a ghost dolphin! But there *is* something alive up there."

Zoey frowned. "They took all the animals away when the park closed."

"I know." Alex continued along the beach. "The octopus led me there. It was like it was being summoned." It had felt like *he* was being summoned too, but what he had to tell her was already unbelievable enough. "When I got up there I found otters feeding something inside one of the old tanks. And when I looked, something looked back."

"Ghost dolphins," Zoey whispered, shivering theatrically.

Alex sighed. Once his best friend got an idea in her head it was almost impossible to shake it loose.

"There was a guard too. I nearly got caught," he said. "Why would there suddenly be a guard at an abandoned aquarium if they weren't hiding something?"

Above the town, the glass house shone dully in the morning light. There was no more green glow. No sign of anything strange at all.

"So what do you think it was?" asked Zoey.

Alex remembered the lengthy, serpentine body curled inside the dark water. The ashy eye that had fixed upon him.

"A monster," he said, though the word fizzed like a lie on his tongue. Last night he had been too scared to think clearly. In the light of day he realized he had felt no malevolence from the creature in the tank. Only its anguish. "I think it wants my help."

Instead, he had run away.

"Are you just trying to distract me with stories to make me feel better?" Zoey asked.

"I swear I'm not making it up."

Zoey stopped dead in her tracks. Crouching, she brushed aside a knot of seaweed at her feet. A large fish lay pale and dead on the sand.

Since the Station was built, they had found hundreds washed up like this. The sea life couldn't survive whatever was being pumped into the water.

"We need to find out exactly what the heck is going on and stop it," Zoey said.

They both wanted to save the bay from whatever was being done to it. But unlike him, Zoey could actually *do* something about it. It was her chemistry set that had discovered an unidentified chemical in the water. As soon as her inventions worked – and he truly believed that one day they would – they would be able to use them to fight back. Alex, with his terror of the water, was hardly any use at all.

His jacket rippled, like drowned cargo was trying to surface from beneath it. Alex groaned and opened the zip. A large plastic bag bulging with water hung from his inside pocket. Kraken was balled up inside like a pair of freshly washed socks.

"You brought the octopus?" said Zoey.

"She started trashing the tank when I tried to leave without her. I know this sounds weird, but I think Kraken came all this way to make me help whatever is in the aquarium."

"That *is* weird." Zoey frowned, before her eyes flicked past him, back the way they had walked. "Though not as weird as *that*."

A cavalcade of crabs had followed them along the beach, red and grey shells glistening in the bright sunlight. Their pointed feet pitter-pattered across the sand as they scuttled in sideways pursuit. Alex stepped to one side to let them pass. The crabs promptly changed direction towards him. When he skipped the other way they simply veered right at him again. They quickly encircled him and raised their claws as if seeking a blessing.

"Don't move," whispered Zoey. "Their eyesight is based on movement."

"That's dinosaurs!"

The crabs appeared expectant, beady eyes fixed intently upon him. Alex shuffled his feet uncertainly.

"Good morning."

The crabs replied by shifting formation around him, moving like synchronized swimmers to form a new shape: a lizard-like head with gaping mouth, sealed inside a solid square. A creature trapped inside a cage.

Or a tank.

"Now do you believe something weird is happening?" Alex asked.

Zoey nodded enthusiastically. "The summoning of a well-choreographed crab army definitely warrants further investigation. Let's go to the aquarium and find out exactly what you saw."

When they arrived, a single watchman was posted at the front gate. He jiggled stiffly from foot to foot as if trying to shake out sand from his trouser leg.

"Same uniform as the guards at the Station," whispered Zoey as they hid behind a tree.

The guards there wore stark black outfits and flat caps. They were always strangers who refused to give their names as they hustled away any of the locals who tried to investigate the mysterious building.

Could the Station be linked to whatever was trapped inside the aquarium?

The thought of approaching that tank again filled him with a bottomless dread. But the voice was in his head again, calling him back with the same desperation as the night before.

"We just have to wait for the right moment," whispered Zoey.

Kraken fumbled her way out of Alex's jacket and parked herself on his shoulder. Just as she had the night before, she arched her body and spat a jet of water towards the guard.

Splop.

The man gazed longingly at the wet patch where the

water had landed. The jiggling of his legs intensified into a writhing shuffle. A second splash of water sent him scurrying into a nearby clump of bushes.

"When you gotta go..." said Zoey, giving Kraken a nod of approval.

They hurried across the driveway and through the hole in the glass wall. There was no sign of any more guards patrolling inside.

The abandoned tanks lost their intimidating stature in the dingy daylight filtering through the walls. Oceanic Avenue appeared merely grimy and sad, a collection of relics left over from a forgotten age.

At the end of the avenue, Alex paused at the doors. Zoey bumped into his back and bundled him through.

Daylight made it no easier to see inside the enormous dolphin tank. The space that had cleared around Alex's hand last night had already closed over. Even where the algae was thinner, the water was too silty to give up its secrets.

"It was in there," Alex insisted, though he was already beginning to doubt himself. He hung back near the doors in case they needed to run.

Zoey brushed her fringe out of her eyes and leaned close to the tank. "I don't see anything."

"I saw it," said Alex as firmly as he could manage. And

he could hear it too – the monster was still there, lingering just out of sight.

"Maybe we need to call it." Zoey tucked her elbows tight to her body and splayed her hands wide like stunted flippers. Then she cleared her throat and squealed like a gale blowing through poorly patched sails.

"It's not a ghost dolphin!"

"We should hold a nautical seance just in case."

A chain rattled on the other side of the aquarium, echoing the length of Oceanic Avenue. A moment later they heard the front doors scraping along the ground. An engine grumbled.

"Hide!"

There was nowhere *to* hide. The space around the dolphin tank had deliberately been left open so nothing would block the view when the dolphins performed. They dithered on the spot for an impossibly long moment as the noise of engines edged along the avenue towards them.

"There, climb into that tank!" said Zoey. A smaller display tank in the shape of a treasure chest stood a little around the curve of the path, accompanied by faded information notices on starfish and coral.

Together they scrambled over the high sides and gasped as they splashed down waist-deep into freezing brown water.

Beside them, the muddy surface stirred. Alex realized they weren't alone in their hiding place. Four sea otters stared at them imploringly from the other side of the tank.

"I told you there were otters!" Alex whispered.

The sound of the engines grew closer. The sides of their hiding place were so coated with scum that they couldn't see out, which at least meant nobody would see *in*. Carefully, Alex wiped a tiny circle of glass clear so he could spy on who had arrived.

Two vehicles pulled up beside the dolphin tank. The first was a long, black classic car, red curtains drawn across the inside of its windows. Close behind it was a battered green four-by-four, mud splattered liberally along its sides.

A chauffeur in driver's cap and gloves hurried out of the first car to open the rear passenger door. Mayor Parch rose regally from his seat, dressed in full mayoral robes: a lush red coat trailing past his short legs to the ground, its collar and sleeves wide and black. A gold chain clattered around his neck as he straightened to full height, which was hardly taller than the roof of the car. He dabbed at his squashed nose with an embroidered handkerchief. Two more guards in black uniforms, a man and a woman, emerged from the car to stand watch.

The man who lifted himself out of the four-by-four

appeared to be the mayor's exact opposite. He was almost as broad as his car, and considerably taller. A frayed and shabby cable-knit jumper clung tightly to a barrel chest and thick arms. Unruly sideburns advanced from a green beanie hat squeezed over his head and stopped just before they reached the corners of his chapped lips. A shark tooth necklace hung around his throat.

"I told you to keep it inside the Station," said the mystery man, looking bitterly around the dilapidated park. "Instead you found the most inconvenient location possible."

The mayor frowned. "You also said to keep it away from the ocean so it can't use its powers. I'd say this fits the bill, wouldn't you, Callis? Better safe than sorry! Maybe if you had been here yourself, we might have discussed it. It wasn't exactly easy smuggling it up here in the dead of night."

Alex remembered the truck from three nights before. It *had* been going to the aquarium!

The other man – Callis – scratched at his sideburns before trying to peer into the big tank in front of him.

"Do you have any idea how much this plan has cost? I broke off an exceptionally lucrative rare animal hunt just to get back here as quickly as I could," he growled. "You don't want to have wasted my time."

The mayor chuckled. "You won't be disappointed."

A click of his fingers sent the guards to the boot of

the car. A full array of diving gear was stored there: wetsuits, flippers and oxygen tanks. The guards quickly changed outfits. Their fins slapped the ground as they approached a heavy metal circular hatch built into a maintenance access unit at the bottom of the tank.

"We kept the filtration system off in case anybody came sniffing around," said Mayor Parch. "Once they unblock it you'll see that everything went exactly as planned."

The divers lugged the hatch away, revealing the mouth of a water-filled pipe that curved up inside the tank. The woman went first, pulling goggles over her eyes and clenching her oxygen mouthpiece between her teeth. She ducked inside and began swimming up the pipe. The other diver promptly followed.

"I told you there was something here," whispered Alex, voice shaking as the cold from the water around his waist crept into his bones.

"Yeah, but you didn't mention the mayor was mixed up in it," Zoey whispered back.

After a minute or so, a mechanical whirring began to sound from the open entrance to the pipe. The water gargled like a blue whale swilling mouthwash. The inside of the tank stirred. Dead leaves and silt were drawn towards the vents and sucked into the filter tunnel to be cleared away.

The divers were spat out inside the tank right near the top – the pipe must have offered passage all the way into the water. They swam to the front. Rapidly they swiped the algae away to expose broad stripes of clean glass. It took moments for them to clear a viewing window, only their bodies blocking the way. Callis stepped eagerly closer.

The water had already cleared. The divers parted, swimming to the surface.

Even though he had known it was there, even though he had already glimpsed it the night before, Alex gasped when he saw what languished inside the tank.

A real-life sea monster.

CHAPTER SIX
THE WATER DRAGON

The creature trapped inside the tank had a long, sinuous body that spiralled away to end in a single fin flared wide like a mermaid's tail. Interlocking plates of armour rounded over its back, scaled in grey and green patchwork. Raw pink scars and pockmarks carved grievous patterns in its flesh.

Mayor Parch and Callis leaned in for a closer look. The creature lifted its mighty head from the protective whorl of its body. It was almost lion-like in shape, short snouted and heavy jawed. Needle-like spines speared from its chin like stalactites. Its eyes, cloudy grey pearls, were set deep in its proud face.

"That's one weird-looking dolphin," whispered Zoey.

Beside them the otters chirped excitedly, bouncing up and down in the muddy water.

Callis scraped the hat off his head and clutched it to his chest. His breath fogged the side of the tank. When he reached to wipe it clear, Alex noticed a vicious scar on his forearm, the healed skin around it seamed and puckered as if some had been torn away.

"It's what you thought?" asked the mayor.

Callis nodded. "The Water Dragon. After all these years."

Alex smothered a gasp. The stories were real. The sea monster – the mythical Water Dragon – was *real*.

"We followed the instructions you left us to the letter," said Mayor Parch. "The creature was pulled into one of the Station intake pipes three days ago. It appeared quite dead at first. I thought you might have over-egged how much of that chemical you told us to put into the bay. Luckily, it began to perk up a little when we got it here."

The creature had been here for three days. Exactly as long as Alex had been having those strange dreams about the aquarium.

"You think I'd mess up the most important part of a plan I've been working on for years?" Callis said, voice oddly hushed. "The dragon was born here. It has had a connection to Haven Bay for centuries. I knew as soon as it sensed the pollution and litter in the water here it would come back to use its powers to try and fix it. And the toxin pumped into the bay from the Station made sure it wouldn't have the strength to leave."

Alex could hardly believe what he was hearing. They had polluted the bay on purpose so they could poison and capture this creature. It *was* the Station that had turned the water sour.

The divers emerged from the filtration pipe, fins slapping against the path as they crossed back to the cars. Alex risked wiping away a little more dirt from the side of their hiding place so he had a better view.

The Water Dragon kept its head raised in the water. The milky brew of its eyes made it appear blind, but Alex knew it had seen him the night before. He felt almost as if it could see him now.

"This *creature*", said Mayor Parch, voice dripping with disdain, "is really as valuable as you say?"

Callis straightened up and crammed his hat back onto his head. "Since humankind first took to the oceans, countless men have died in pursuit of this beast. Three decades of my life have led me to this moment."

Mayor Parch simply blinked. "So that's a yes?"

"You should understand," continued Callis, gaze still fixed on the dragon, "there is no known creature on the planet as powerful as the Water Dragon. It controls the balance of the world's oceans. It strives to keep safe every living soul that relies on the sea to survive. And make no mistake, that includes us too. If the oceans die, so does mankind. Whoever controls the Water Dragon will wield immeasurable power. There are plenty who will pay handsomely to possess this beast."

The mayor rubbed his hands together with delight. "You remember our deal? You wouldn't have caught it without me letting you build the Station!"

Callis finally tore his eyes away from the tank. Although he tried to hide it, the contempt in his expression was plain to see.

"I'll put the word out," he said. "It may take a day or two. I'll be in touch with the details."

The man turned away and strode briskly to his car. Once the four-by-four had retreated through the archway, Parch stepped closer to the tank.

"You, little lizard, are going to make me a rich man."

The Water Dragon turned its cloudy eyes upon the mayor and lifted its head higher. Drawing a breath of water, its throat inflated like a beach ball, spiked air sacs puffing out wide. Mayor Parch stumbled away in alarm, trod on the hem of his robes, and tumbled flat onto his back.

Alex stifled a laugh. The dragon's eyes flicked towards his hiding place. Its lips drew back to reveal what might have been a sharp-toothed smile.

The chauffeur rushed across the path to pull the floundering mayor to his feet. Huffing, Mayor Parch allowed himself to be led to the back seat of the car.

As soon as it had manoeuvred through the archway, Alex and Zoey climbed out of the treasure-chest tank. The otters clambered out after them and the group approached together. The Water Dragon's ruff was slowly deflating, air bubbles trailing from its scaly nostrils.

"I can't believe it's real," said Zoey. "The legends make it sound bigger. And scarier."

Alex stood a few steps away from the glass. It seemed scary enough to him. Although the dragon was trapped safely inside the tank, he still felt like its prey. He peered deep into the Water Dragon's eyes and wondered about everything it must have seen in the centuries before it was trapped in the old Haven Bay aquarium. The dragon watched him closely in return.

"That creepy Callis guy said it has powers," Zoey continued eagerly. "Do you reckon it has laser eyes? Dragons are supposed to fly, aren't they? Oh, maybe it can poop boats!"

Alex struggled to find the right words. "They weakened it so it couldn't use its powers. It's...diminished."

It *should* have been bigger. Somehow Alex knew that

captivity had lessened the dragon. Its scales seemed loose and cracked as mismatched paving stones, its skin sallow and sagging. If it could just breathe, if it just had the *space*, it would fill its powerful frame and resume its true, gargantuan size.

"You heard them!" said Zoey. "That's why the mayor let the Station be built in the first place. It was all so they could trap the dragon."

Alex closed his eyes. The dragon's voice nagged at the back of his mind. It seemed muted, as if struggling to be heard from beneath fathoms of water.

Inside the tank, the dragon whipped its tail upwards, spraying water over the top. It splashed across Alex's skin. Images flashed across his mind: people running along a beach; a towering wave; teeth emerging from the sea.

Alex staggered away. "Did you see that?"

Zoey, soaked to the skin, blinked at him blankly. "It was hard to miss the unwanted shower."

Kraken reached a pair of arms to the glass and shifted her skin to the same green the dragon had glowed the night before. Answering light shimmered faintly through the dragon's scales. The octopus grabbed Alex's collar and pulled his face towards the side of the tank.

The Water Dragon brushed its spiny muzzle against the glass. Its mouth opened, revealing rows of needle-like teeth around a soft pink palate. It was trying to tell him something, to share centuries-worth of experience.

"It needs to be free," Alex said. "That must be why the octopus is here. And the otters and the birds. It called them to help it escape."

The octopus cycled through a rainbow of colours, as if relieved they had finally understood.

Alex nodded, finally sure. "If it stays here, it will die. It needs to get back to the ocean before they can sell it."

It was plainly an impossible task. They were half a mile from the sea and at the pinnacle of a steep hill. The Water Dragon was large enough that they'd need a truck to transport it.

"How do you know what it wants?"

"I just..."

He remembered Grandma holding him back from the water's edge, sadness etched into the lines of her face.

"I just know it's the right thing to do," he said.

Zoey simply nodded her agreement, calculating cogs already turning and clicking behind her eyes.

"It sounds like we don't have long," she said.

"So we move fast," said Alex. "Before its power can fall into the wrong hands."

Inside the tank, the Water Dragon bowed its head to him, before twining around itself in a watchful braid.

CHAPTER SEVEN

ATTACK OF THE WATER SAUSAGES

Rescuing the Water Dragon was a matter of urgency, but so was making it home for his afternoon shift with enough time to wash off the cold sludge that clung to his skin and squeaked between his toes. The otters trailed behind Alex and Zoey in a neat line as they crept out of the aquarium and towards town.

The sound of chimes jangled an approach behind them. The otters managed to scurry up Alex's trouser legs – two on each side – before Grandpa pulled alongside them in the ice cream van.

"Why are you wet?" he growled, leaning out of the window. "You know you en't allowed in the water!"

"There was a rainstorm," blurted Alex.

Grandpa turned his gaze to the clear blue sky overhead. "A really *quick* rainstorm."

Thankfully the conversation was interrupted by the arrival of Mr Ballister, one of the local retired fishermen, who plucked out his false teeth as he approached the serving window.

"Do you have any ice cream that isn't too cold?" he asked.

They took the opportunity to escape, Alex waddling awkwardly while the otters clung to his legs.

Eventually they reached Neptune's Bounty, stopping just before the window so Alex's dad wouldn't see them.

"We need to find out exactly what Callis and the mayor are planning," said Zoey. "Then we can work out how to stop them."

"How are we going to do that?"

"We break into the mayor's office."

"And how are we going to do *that?*"

A mischievous smile slinked across Zoey's face. "I'll think of something."

"Can you take Kraken with you?" Alex asked, holding out the watery pouch with the octopus inside. "If she keeps jumping out of her tank Dad is going to notice."

Zoey rolled her eyes. "And he'll just ignore four sea otters." She snatched the bag. "I have an old fish tank she can use."

She set off along the high street towards the boatyard, Kraken waving goodbye with two front arms. That left Alex with the otters gathered around his feet.

"Uh...shoo?"

The animals lined up and peered at him expectantly.

"No, that's the opposite of shoo."

First, it had been Kraken so readily allowing Alex to take her home. Then the procession of crabs that had cornered him on the beach. And now this. In the last two days – ever since the Water Dragon had been captive – he seemed to have become a minor celebrity to sea animals.

There seemed little choice but to let the otters follow him around the side of the shop. K-pop pounded from the garage where Bridget would be in the middle of another workout. He opened the side door to the house and tiptoed inside. Together they hurried up the stairs.

The otters flocked into the bathroom. Alex rushed after them and locked the door.

"Wait over there," he commanded, pointing the otters to the cobwebbed space under the sink. To his surprise they obeyed, pushing their noses together as if having a private conversation.

Alex peeled off his sodden clothes and set the shower running. The bathroom quickly filled with steam, fogging the mirrors and windows.

He had just worked his armpits into a soapy lather when the first otter pushed between his legs to reach the stream of the shower. Alex wobbled away and almost tripped over two more lying on their backs and juggling a bottle of bubble bath between them.

"Stop that!"

His lunge to catch the bottle only succeeded in knocking it against the side of the tub. The cap broke off and bright pink bubble bath sluiced around his feet. He slipped over and landed hard against the taps. As he scrambled to right himself, feet sliding in the pink slick, the remaining otter leaped onto his back. In a flailing scramble to break his fall he grabbed the shower hose and yanked it away from the wall. High pressure made the hose whip and thrash, dousing the walls and ceiling with water.

Thick white foam boiled up out of the bath. The otters frolicked through the fragrant froth, chirping wildly. Alex pounced onto the lashing shower hose and wrestled it like a prize python as bubbles rose around his neck.

Finally, he snatched the shower head and lunged for the taps to cut off the flow of water. The otters each stood up on their hind legs to fix him with a reproachful glare.

"Stop it!" Alex ordered.

There was a surge of power in the words. He felt his voice move through the water that soaked the floor and connect with the otters, as if it was translating into a language they understood – the same as when the dragon had tried to speak to him. The otters obeyed immediately, stopping in their tracks.

There was a sharp rapping on the door.

"Everything okay in there?" came Dad's voice. "I've been hearing a lot of strange splashing noises."

"Nothing to worry about!" Alex called back, wiping bubbles away from his mouth. "I just have diarrhoea!"

"Oh, I see," came the reply. "Make sure you clean up after yourself, okay?"

Dad's footsteps departed hastily down the stairs.

Alex hurried to dry himself – and the floor, and the walls, and the ceiling – before wrapping himself in his dressing gown.

"Now listen up," he told the otters, trying to grasp the connection in his mind. "I don't know what's going on here, but if you insist on following me, you're going to do *exactly* what I say. We're going into my bedroom where you will *not* cause any more trouble. Understood?"

Each otter lifted a front paw to its head and chirruped, in what looked suspiciously like salutes to a superior officer.

As soon as the bathroom door was open and Alex was satisfied the coast was clear, he urged them to move. The otters marched in two orderly pairs ahead of him, straight across the landing and into his bedroom.

The animals could understand him. Between the octopus, the crabs and now the otters, it couldn't be a coincidence. Maybe if he could harness the power to make them obey him all the time, he could at least avoid his dad finding out about all this.

A low growl rumbled from inside his bedroom. Alex entered to find the otters frozen in their tracks. Up on the bed, Chonkers the cat had become a rigid arch of startled hair.

"There's no need to be frightened," Alex cooed, unsure if he needed to soothe Chonkers or the otters. "We can all get along."

Even if the cat could understand him, he knew she would pay him no attention. By now Chonkers had fluffed up to the size of a beach ball. She peeled her lips back over her teeth and hissed. In return, the otters trilled and gathered into a tight defensive formation.

"I'm sure we can settle this without a fight," pleaded Alex.

The cat yowled like an air-raid siren and pounced.

Chonkers was an absolute unit of a cat, but the otters had numbers on their side. While one of them remained in the firing line, another dodged and plucked the cat up by her armpits. Rolling onto its back, it used its rear legs to launch Chonkers into the air.

The otters quickly formed a circle to juggle the cat between them. Front paws deftly caught the cat while back legs acted like powerful catapults. Chonkers wailed indignantly through the air with every throw.

Alex waded into the circle and tried to catch the cat as she sailed past. The otters warbled, a lilting sound suspiciously like laughter, as they ensured the airborne cat remained just out of Alex's grasping reach. He strained for the power he had felt in the bathroom, but it was like a rope running through his hands too quickly to grasp.

Finally, Chonkers caught herself by lashing out to sink needle claws into the flesh of Alex's knee.

"Ow!" screamed Alex, tumbling to the floor. "I'm trying to help you, idiot!"

The cat used the opening to strike at the nearest otter, boxing its face with both front paws.

The otters regrouped and pinned Chonkers down, tickling the cat's exposed belly. She howled in dismay and turned pleading eyes on Alex.

The bedroom door banged open. Bridget stepped inside to survey the tangle of otter, feline and human.

"What the *flip* is going on in here?" she said.

Alex was too exhausted to even attempt a lie. "I have a small problem."

Bridget groaned and stomped into the room. Her biceps

bulged as she easily scooped the otters away from the cat and up into her arms.

Across the landing, the top stair creaked. Footsteps rapidly approached the open door. Bridget whipped the otters behind her back.

"We heard banging," said Dad, peering into the room.

"And some kind of piteous mewling," added Grandpa beside him.

"That was Alex," said Bridget quickly. "He was attempting a single press-up."

"You know that was a silly thing to do." Dad tutted and shook his head. "Come down and watch the shop as soon as you're dry."

Before they left, Grandpa scanned the room with narrowed eyes and fixed Alex with a searching look.

When the coast was clear Bridget released the otters from her iron grip. They flocked onto the bed to bundle together against the pillows.

"I could have chipped a nail!" admonished Bridget.

"Why did you help me hide them?" Alex asked.

Bridget sighed and took a moment to reply. "As if I want you grounded for ever so you're *always* here." She scooped up Chonkers. "You're coming to my try-out at the gym tomorrow, right? I want you to see me *crush* those little boys."

"I'll be there."

Chonkers had just enough time to glare daggers at the otters before the door closed.

Alex slumped onto the bed. "You can understand me?" he asked.

The otters chirruped in response.

"And I did *something* back there to make you actually listen to me. I just don't know how to do it again."

He had discovered so much in the last twenty-four hours, yet it still seemed like half the story was hidden from him. Closing his eyes, he pictured the Water Dragon in his mind. The sinuous, armoured length of its body. Its shrewd, famished face. It wanted to tell him everything he didn't know. Alex just wasn't sure if he was ready to hear it.

CHAPTER EIGHT

THE GREAT SEAGULL STICK-UP

The next day, Alex and Zoey waited across the road for the mayor to leave his office for lunch. A swarm of seagulls circled above, forcing Zoey to cradle her lunch close to her chest and swing an arm at any bird that strayed too close.

Before Mayor Parch took over, the mayor's office had been a single room above the *Chipping Forecast* chip shop on the high street. Anybody could visit for a chat while enjoying a steaming portion of scampi or a chip butty.

Mayor Parch changed that on his first day. He shut down Haven Bay library and moved his office into the building instead. Apparently he believed its grand stone columns carved with mystifying Latin phrases were more befitting of his new-found status. The entire length of the roof bristled with spikes to ward off seagulls.

It looked like a fortress. Alex and Zoey needed to find a way inside.

The mayor's personal study was at the back of the building. Miss Kedge, his secretary, served as gatekeeper. She spent her entire day at the front desk, steely eyes fixed on the entrance, poised to chase off anybody who even considered disturbing Mayor Parch.

They crossed the street and hid behind one of the columns. Through a window they could see Miss Kedge in position. From her appearance it was hard to believe there was anything threatening about her. She was small enough that only her head was visible above the desk. Glasses sat low on her pointed nose and her hair was pulled up into a neat bun.

The locals told a different story. Allegedly she had tackled Mrs Leech to the ground when she tried to complain about the bay becoming so filthy, and bodily ejected a local reporter when he asked for more information about the Station. Mr Ballister swore blind she had come at him with a letter opener when he requested a selfie with the historical mayoral busts that decorated the office.

"I could burst a sewage pipe and stink them out," said Zoey. "Or I know where to find a particularly large wasp nest and a catapult."

"Let's call those Plans F and G," replied Alex. The problem was that they didn't yet have a Plan A, B or C.

Zoey unwrapped her lunch, a clutch of perfectly round steamed buns. The bread had been decorated with animals from the Chinese Zodiac: a tiger, a rabbit and a dragon.

"Dad even has to be an artist on my baozi," she huffed. "He's such a show-off."

An octopus arm crept from inside her jacket to reach for the buns. Zoey opened the jacket wide to reveal Kraken climbing from her bag of water.

"She kept bashing against the tank until I gave up and brought her with me."

"I told you she can be surprisingly persuasive," said Alex.

A seagull took advantage of their distraction and snatched a bun from Zoey's grasp. She lunged after it, but the gull wheeled out of reach and away towards the water.

"That better not be Anil's stupid bird!" she shouted.

Another gull swooped at the buns, forcing Zoey to shove one whole into her mouth and throw the other to Alex. He chomped on the bun just as a seagull dived for it, the delicious flavour of barbecue pork flooding his mouth.

"So much for art," Zoey mumbled through her mouthful.

A smile broke across Alex's face. He watched the

seagulls devour the hijacked bun. They could be a nuisance, but maybe there was a way to turn that to their advantage.

The mayor's long, black car pulled up outside the office. The chauffeur had just enough time to fling open the rear door before Parch left the building and climbed straight into the back seat.

"Now's our chance," said Alex as soon as the car had rounded the corner and disappeared.

"There's no way we'll get past her," said Zoey.

They flinched back behind the column as Miss Kedge glanced up from her desk.

"I have a plan," said Alex. He checked there was nobody nearby, before clearing his throat and shouting at the top of his voice, "Hey, seagulls, we need your help!"

He *knew* they could understand him. If he just commanded them with enough authority, he could find that connection again and make them obey.

A single seagull drifted overhead and spattered droppings on the pavement at his feet.

"Are you feeling okay?" asked Zoey.

Grumbling under his breath, Alex reached behind the column. There were other ways to attract seagulls.

"Plan B," he said, retrieving a hidden dustbin and opening the lid. The putrid smell of rubbish washed over them.

"This might seem a bit weird," he said.

"Weirder than talking to seagulls?"

Before she could even finish the question, Alex lifted the bin off the ground and upended it over his head. Slime splattered his shoulders and soaked his hair. Blackened banana skins and chewed chicken bones fell like rancid hail. A mushy napkin plastered itself across his face.

Zoey gaped at him. "What the heck did you do that for?"

Alex clawed the napkin away from his mouth and pointed to the sky. The frantic squawking of seagulls, distant just moments before, was rapidly growing closer.

"I'm going to cause a diversion."

Miss Kedge's greatest talent was peering *up* from her desk while still unmistakably looking *down* her nose at whoever she faced.

It would have been difficult for her to ignore Alex's entrance. Every footstep sounded like wet underwear being wrung out over a sink. Brown juice welled out of his shoes onto the plush red carpet. He walked far enough inside to ensure he was making a mess while still being able to hold the door open behind him.

The secretary aggressively cleared her throat. "Can I help you, young man?"

It was surprisingly troublesome to speak when he was trying not to breathe through his nose. "I'm here to complain about the seagulls."

Miss Kedge rose slowly from her desk. "What seagulls?"

Alex threw the door open as wide as he could. "*These* seagulls."

A hurricane of white and grey feathers fumed through the doorway. The seagulls screeched and yapped madly as they tumbled over each other in pursuit of the noxious morsels splattered across Alex's clothes.

Miss Kedge howled and launched herself over the desk, swinging her handbag furiously at the swarming birds.

"As you can see, they are clearly a menace!" Alex shouted over the cacophony of seagulls while also trying to protect his face from the worst of their razor-sharp beaks and grasping talons.

Regaining her composure, Miss Kedge dashed around the room to throw open the windows. Alex watched to make sure she hurried through to the study to open the window behind the mayor's desk.

"Oh, the smell! His Lordship does not care for foul odours!" she cried. "We have to get these bird-brained hoodlums out of here before His Lordship returns!"

Alex made sure to wave his arms hard enough that slime and filth spattered across the room. The seagulls chased it eagerly, wings battering the walls and claws tearing at the carpet.

Miss Kedge retrieved a long, pink feather duster from behind her desk and chased the birds around the room. Alex peered inside the mayor's study. The open doorway gave him a clear view of Parch's desk. Rows of plinths flanked it, each displaying a grey stone bust of the town's most famous mayors, forming two lines of old men frowning resentfully at the office.

From outside, hands appeared on the window frame. A foot hooked over the sill. Zoey heaved herself up and through the window Miss Kedge had so helpfully opened, face burning red with the effort. She rolled inside and dropped onto the soft carpet, throwing Alex a wink. Kraken was perched blithely on her shoulder.

"Not the tapestry!" howled Miss Kedge as the gulls continued to fly amok.

Alex silently congratulated himself on a successful diversion.

Meanwhile, Zoey edged along the line of busts towards the desk. One of the wooden plinths wobbled as she passed, the stone head atop it swaying precariously. She grabbed it just in time to keep it from falling.

The desperate lunge was noisy enough to catch Miss Kedge's attention. She broke off her chase and turned towards the study door.

"Ow, my eye!" screamed Alex, clutching theatrically at his face as if he had been viciously pecked. "I'm going to sue this town!"

The secretary rushed across to him. "There's no need for lawyers to get involved! You'd be *amazed* what they can do with glass eyes these days!"

Inside the study, Zoey reached the mayor's desk. She flung open drawers and pulled out reams of paper and notes, riffling quickly through the pages. They needed anything that would reveal the details of what Callis and Mayor Parch were planning to do with the Water Dragon.

By now the seagulls had snaffled most of the scraps. A few waddled imperiously across the lavish carpet in search of more, which made them easy targets for a whack with the feather duster. One by one they began to make for the open windows and freedom.

"And don't come back!" Miss Kedge screeched after them.

Zoey had reached the bottom drawer, which contained another pile of papers. After scanning and discarding a few pages, her face lit up. She began shovelling the mess back into the desk. They would have to hope anything out of place would be blamed on the plundering seagulls.

Once the drawers were all closed, Zoey hurried back

towards the window. In her haste she collided with one of the plinths and sent a stone head thudding to the carpet.

Miss Kedge dropped the feather duster and rushed towards the study door. Zoey was stranded behind the plinth with nowhere else to hide.

Just as the secretary reached the office door, Kraken hoisted herself up to stretch all eight arms wide across Zoey's face. The octopus's blue skin drained instantly of colour, becoming the same blanched grey as the other busts, darker patches approximating facial features.

Miss Kedge studied the room closely. Zoey remained completely still, her body hidden behind the wooden plinth. Her camouflaged face was indistinguishable from the stone heads on display.

Finally, the secretary turned back to Alex. Her hair had escaped its bun to spray out in frazzled tresses. "Look at the mess you've made!"

Slimy footprints were drying to a crust on the red carpet. White feathers and whiter spatters of droppings had been left everywhere by the gulls.

A final glance through to the study revealed Zoey climbing safely out of the window. Alex puffed up his chest and tried not to choke on his own odour.

"Look at the mess those birds made of *me*! You'll be hearing from my lawyer!"

The secretary was struck by a moment of speechlessness that allowed Alex to escape onto the street. He hurried towards the sea wall and down the steps onto the beach. Zoey was waiting for him there.

"Did you find it?" he asked.

"I got something even better!" From behind her back she whipped out the mayor's plush red coat.

"You stole his costume?"

"I thought it might suit me." Zoey threw the coat around her shoulders. It hardly reached past her knees. "He really *is* short."

"Please tell me you found what you actually broke in there for."

Zoey nodded. "I have good news and bad news."

"Good news first."

"Now they've caught the dragon they've stopped pumping chemicals into the water."

"It won't reverse the damage they've already done," said Alex. "What's the bad news?"

"They're putting the word out about the Water Dragon so they can hold an auction. Tomorrow night at the aquarium," said Zoey. "The mayor did a deal to help Raze Callis – that's his full name, apparently – catch the dragon, so they're going to split the money fifty-fifty."

"The same night as the Water Dragon ceremony,"

said Alex, clenching his fists. "They're going to use it as cover."

Zoey nodded. "We need to get the dragon the heck out of there before tomorrow night."

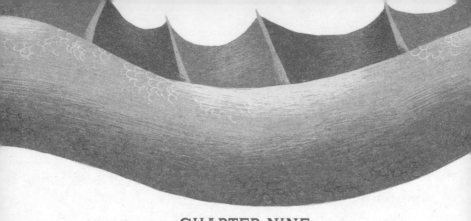

CHAPTER NINE

HOW TO ATTAIN YOUR DRAGON

The relocated library was inside an old fishery warehouse. Lopsided shelves ran the length of the long metal walls, packed with books slowly turning brown and wrinkled in the inescapably damp space. Wooden picnic tables and colourful sandcastle buckets to catch the ceiling drips were scattered around the middle of the warehouse. The sour smell of fish lingered on the air – although it was almost eclipsed by the smell of Alex, despite their quick visit to the boatyard first so he could clean off the gunk and rubbish (and so they could drop Kraken off for some tank time).

Still, the poor conditions at the library didn't keep people away. Alex and Zoey found it full of children absorbed almost as deeply in books as they were in the oversized beanbag chairs. Older people sat at boxy desktop computers or simply read magazines and newspapers. A group of people were busy making Brineblood scarecrows, stuffing shredded paper into tattered old shirts.

"Why are we here?" asked Alex as he followed Zoey between the bookshelves.

"You can find anything you need to know at the library," she insisted. "And we need as much information about Callis and the aquarium park as we can get."

First they sat at a computer and typed *Raze Callis* into a search engine. The first result was a recent news story. The headline read: *Notorious Poacher Escapes Jail Time.*

Raze Callis, the lead suspect in almost one hundred poaching cases, was found not guilty on all counts due to lack of evidence. Callis (47) was accused of killing some of the world's most endangered animals after entering multiple protected areas of ocean environment. He is best known as a prolific marine hunter, often recruited by the rich and the famous to lead hunting expeditions.

Soon they found images of Callis posing with animals he had killed, alongside more news stories and interviews on hunting websites. Every link used the same main image: Callis standing proudly beside an enormous shark hanging from a hook by its tail, mouth wide open and bloodied.

"At least the shark took a bite out of him first," said Zoey, pointing to Callis's bandaged arm in the photo.

Alex remembered the puckered scar on Callis's forearm, as if skin had been torn away.

"We know he's planning to sell the Water Dragon rather than kill it," said Alex. "But I could sense that it will die in captivity."

Zoey clicked angrily to shut all their tabs. "How dare they? The dragon must be thousands of years old! I didn't know anything could even live that long."

"The ocean is a sanctuary for ancient things," said Alex. "The oldest lobster ever caught was one hundred and forty years old. Greenland sharks live for four hundred years. There's a jellyfish that can live *for ever*. The sea is a different world. It has different rules."

They left the computer and went deeper into the library. Hidden away under a rusty conveyor belt was a low counter of stained, dented metal. The light overhead flickered erratically. Zoey tapped a bell on the counter – *ding!* – and waited approximately one-fifth of a second before she hit it again even harder.

DING!

A hunched figure unfolded himself from a low doorway cut into the metal of the wall. Thick glasses magnified his eyes; a long nose ended in a pitted round lump like a sea urchin shell. The elbows of his tweed jacket had been worn to a mirror sheen.

"Good afternoon, Sugden," said Zoey brightly.

"Hello, Miss Wu," the librarian managed to reply in a continuous sigh. "What are you accidentally blowing up today?"

Zoey clasped her hands together on top of the counter and leaned closer. "Before I give you my request, you must give me your word you won't tell another living soul what I ask."

"I fear you gravely overestimate how much I care about any single record you might seek in the town archive," Sugden drawled. "And, indeed, how many people I converse with on a daily basis."

Zoey slapped her hands on the counter. "Right then! We need to see blueprints and plans for the old aquarium house."

Sugden's practised coolness was betrayed by an eyebrow twitch. "Funny...I know exactly where they are." He ducked through the low doorway and reappeared moments later with a roll of large, thick documents.

"That was fast," said Zoey.

"They happened to be to hand," replied the librarian.

They retreated to the quietest corner of the library and unfurled the documents across the table. The pages appeared to Alex to show little more than impenetrable grids of straight lines and a labyrinth of looping circles.

"That's the aquarium?"

Zoey huffed an exasperated sigh. "It makes sense when you know what to look for. See, that's the dragon's tank," she said, jabbing a finger at a hexagonal shape near the centre of the page. "And that's the entrance."

With guidance, the blueprint began to give up its secrets. Oceanic Avenue and the placement of the tanks became clear.

"It feels like we're planning to rob the place," said Alex.

"We kind of *are*," countered Zoey, sounding a little too pleased about the idea. "It's going to be a heist."

Although he was no expert, Alex thought heists were supposed to involve breaking into a bank vault to steal all the gold bars or sneaking into a casino to pocket wads of cash. He had never heard of a heist to rescue a mythical sea creature.

The blueprints did little to dispel the nagging suspicion that it was a ridiculous idea. The park was huge. The Water

Dragon was huge. Callis was a famous poacher who also happened to be huge.

But the Water Dragon needed his help. Alex was sure of it. So the least he could do was try.

"If the auction is tomorrow night, we don't have much time to make a plan."

Zoey nodded, studying the blueprints closely. "The auction could work to our advantage. It'll be busy enough that we can disguise ourselves to get inside and the guards won't notice. Once we're in I can use my drone to keep track of everybody so we don't get caught."

"If it still catches fire I think it might draw too much attention."

"It's so close to working properly," she said. "I just need to iron out a few more problems."

"Then we actually have to get the dragon out of the tank. It must weigh a tonne," added Alex. "And then we have to get it past the guests and out of the building."

"Your shop sells those sliding mats, right?" she asked. "Just add soap and water."

"You want us to *slide* the dragon away?"

"You got a better way?" Zoey ran her fingertips over the page. "There's another problem. See this?"

Alex squinted at the kaleidoscope of criss-crossing lines and technical jargon. "Explain it to me like I'm five."

The idea seemed increasingly hopeless as Zoey explained how the dragon's tank was built and how difficult it would be for them to get inside. It was too tall to climb, the glass too sheer and slick. There was only one other way: the filtration pipe they had seen the divers use. Alex glared at the blueprints as if they might surrender an easier solution he was missing.

"Who would've guessed that smuggling a mythical sea creature out of a heavily guarded glass aquarium house on a hill would be so difficult?" said Zoey.

"There's no way we can do this by ourselves," said Alex. "We need to put together a team."

Somebody to go through the filtration pipe and tie a rope around the dragon. Somebody else strong enough to lift it over the top of the tank. Puzzle pieces of a plan began to slot together in his mind.

Zoey didn't try to hide her scepticism when he outlined his idea. "Do we really have to get other people involved?"

"Do you have a better idea?"

"We load a catapult with ants and— "

Alex rolled up the blueprints. "It's the best chance we have."

"We still need a way to get into the park before the auction," said Zoey.

"I might have a way," Alex replied, studying the mayor's coat slung across the back of her chair and remembering how Kraken had disguised herself.

"All right, so no more toxins in the bay means it's safe for the dragon again. If we *do* manage to get it out of the park, how the heck do we transport it there?"

Now Alex hesitated. *That* was definitely a major hole in the plan.

They returned the blueprints to the desk, dinging the bell to get Sugden's attention. The librarian sloped out to reclaim the documents.

Zoey stopped him before he could shuffle away again. "Why was it so easy for you to find the plans? Usually you take ages."

"A librarian takes exactly as long as is necessary," sniffed Sugden. "Today it just so happens that you were the *second* person to request these documents."

Zoey reached into her pocket and slid a twenty pence piece across the counter. "Who else asked for the plans?"

"I had no interest in learning their name."

A stack of books rested on the side of the counter. Zoey casually began nudging it towards the edge. "It would be a shame if something bad happened to these."

"He was a grubby fellow, dirty jumper and ill-advised sideburns!" whimpered Sugden, lunging to rescue the books.

"Tall enough to hit his head on the lights!"

"That sounds like Callis," said Alex.

Zoey spun away from the counter. "Why would he need blueprints for the aquarium?"

Alex shook his head. There had to be more to Callis's plans than they realized. "Maybe we have even less time than we thought."

"Okay, we go with your idea." Zoey grinned. "Let's recruit a rescue squad."

CHAPTER TEN

THE DRAGON TUNNELS

A carpet of gold shimmered in the concrete bowl of the fountain in the town square, coins thrown by tourists past wishing for good fortune.

Perched on the stone rim, Anil tossed a length of string into the water before winding it back up on a spool. Forlornly, he studied the end of his makeshift line.

"What are you doing?" Alex asked.

"Fishing for pirate treasure."

A horseshoe-shaped magnet was tied to the end of the string. It dripped into Anil's lap as he prepared to cast the line again.

"Coins aren't even magnetic," said Zoey.

"*Old* coins are. This fountain has been here for years, right?

There must be pieces of eight or doubloons or something." A rusty brown coin clung to the end of the magnet. Anil reeled it up and brandished it triumphantly. "See!"

Zoey peered closer. "That's a penny."

"Oh." Anil flicked it back into the water. "Are *any* of the legends I've read about this place actually true?"

Alex and Zoey exchanged a look – the biggest legend of all had just turned out to be fact.

"I was messaging my brother about—"

Anil was cut off by a scoop of strawberry ice cream splatting onto his head. Pinch squawked from above, pleased with this latest gift.

"This has to stop!" said Anil, scraping the mess out of his hair.

Zoey offered him a stained tissue from her pocket. "There are worse things a bird could drop on your head."

It was the day before the Water Dragon ceremony and the square was filled with Brineblood effigies: hemp sacks stuffed with hay formed lumpen bodies; scuffed footballs and mouldy pumpkins were scrawled with marker-pen faces. It felt like they were being watched from every direction.

Market stalls and street decorations were being set up outside the shops. Tourists might not be coming for the beach any more, but there was still hope they would turn up for the ceremony. The festivities would provide the perfect cover for the auction at the aquarium. Nobody would question the arrival of any strange or unsavoury visitors.

"You really like all the local stories, don't you?" asked Alex.

Anil eagerly nodded his head. "My dad bought me a book of legends from your shop! I thought we were going to investigate them together, but he's always too busy at work. If I can find something really amazing, he'll *have* to come exploring with me."

"I think we might be able to help with that."

That was enough to pique Anil's interest. He listened intently while Alex outlined what they had discovered in the aquarium, why the Station was really built and what Callis was planning to do with the Water Dragon.

"You're telling me that the creature *he* was hunting," Anil said, pointing to the nearby Brineblood scarecrows, "is actually real?"

Alex nodded. "We have to rescue it. And we need your help."

"I knew it!" Anil whooped, before an entire battered sausage hit him in the face. "I'm vegetarian!" he shouted at Pinch as the seagull alighted on the rim of the fountain beside him and nipped the boy's elbow affectionately.

"Hey!"

A burly, sunburned tourist in a tight vest was storming

along the high street towards them. An empty sausage-shaped sheath of greasy paper was still clutched in his fist.

"It was the bird!" Anil cried, springing away from the fountain and breaking into a run as Pinch took off again. Alex and Zoey had little choice but to follow Anil or face the tourist's hungry wrath.

"You really need to train your seagull," puffed Alex.

The chase took them towards the harbour. Old fishing boats, abandoned years before, slanted together along rickety jetties. Thick bands of green and yellow seaweed had grown over the wood, binding the rusty crafts in place. Anil ran to the end of a jetty and beckoned for them to follow.

"I can't go into the water," said Alex, screeching to a halt.

"You don't have to. The tide is out."

The sea had peeled away from the shore, leaving a swathe of brown beach strewn with seaweed and washed-up litter. A long breakwater of stacked stones stretched out from the near side of the beach, only its tip reaching the waterline.

The tourist was rapidly catching them up, face bright red and fists clenched. "You'll pay for stealing my sausage!" he bellowed.

"Okay, so let's go!" said Alex.

They jumped onto the sand, which formed a path towards the base of the cliffs on the far curve of the bay. Alex looked nervously at the distant water, imagining it spotting him there and rushing in to seize him. But he also didn't much fancy being caught by the man hot on their heels.

"The caves!" said Anil. "We can hide in there."

Trapped underneath rock. The tide rising. Light fading to darkness. Grandma had always forbidden Alex from going anywhere near the dragon tunnels.

"They're not safe!" Zoey shouted, as if she had read his mind.

Anil pointed to the foot of the cliffs. "I found a place."

They were chased across the width of the bay, craggy rock rising to form the cliffs ahead of them. A headland pushed out at the lowest point, cut short where the gnawing sea had broken it off years before. It used to be the part of town where the fishermen lived. All that remained was the old church, half of it collapsed over the edge, pointed spire teetering. One day it would tumble away and be swallowed by the waves.

"There's the cave entrance!" said Anil.

Past the headland, spears of rock jutted from the sand like ancient tusks. A low opening bored into the cliff face. Anil hurried inside.

Alex screeched to a halt. "I can't go in there."

"You also can't stay out here." Zoey planted her hands on his back and propelled him into the cave mouth.

The tourist stopped in front of the cave, peering uncertainly into the darkness. "Get back out here!"

"No thanks," Zoey called back.

"I'm really sorry about your sausage!" Anil added.

The tourist gave up, turning away to slope back towards town. "First the beach turns out to be a tip, and now this," he grumbled.

"We should probably wait until we're sure he's really gone," said Anil.

The air inside the cave was cold and damp. Gnarled stalactites dripped from the soaring cavern ceiling and unseen creatures chirped inside swathes of shadow. It was so much larger than Alex had expected. If the stories were true, it was easy to imagine the Water Dragon hiding here while Brineblood besieged the bay all those years ago.

A stack of multi-levelled rock rose up at the back of the cavern. Anil went ahead and began climbing.

"Is it safe?" asked Alex. The cavern picked up his voice and cast it bounding around the walls.

Anil pointed further up the platform. The rock sloped up and away from the ground to form a higher terrace. "That part is always dry, even when the tide is up. You'd just be trapped until it goes out again." He kept climbing. "It's weird how everybody here is so scared of the caves. As soon as I read the stories I *had* to go exploring."

Alex imagined the cavern entrance slipping beneath the rising waves, the light blotted to nothing. He shivered. It would be so easy to get lost in here and never be found.

"Let's just leave," whispered Zoey as soon as Anil was out of earshot.

"We need him for the plan."

"We haven't even told him what it is yet and we're already stuck inside a stinking cave!"

Alex moved to block her escape. "Why don't you like Anil?"

Zoey's face flushed. "He's always sucking up to you."

"I think he's just being friendly."

"You're *my* friend," Zoey said, sharply enough that her voice echoed. "He can't just turn up and take you away from me!"

Alex blinked. He had thought his best friend's urge to protect him was her natural bravery compensating for his fear of the water. It had always made him worry that she would get sick of him being such a coward. He had never even thought that Zoey might be scared of losing him.

"You'll always be my best friend," he told her. "Making new friends won't change that."

For once, she wouldn't meet his eye. "How do you know?"

Alex held up his arms. "You always believe in me, always stand up for me, whether I'm too scared to go for a paddle or asking you to help me steal a mythical sea creature that turns out to be real. There's no way I could do any of this without you."

"I *am* a misunderstood genius." Zoey looked at him and grinned. "All right, I'll give him a chance."

Slimy rocks underfoot forced them to pick their way carefully forwards. Anil offered his hand to help Zoey up. After hesitating for a moment, she took it and climbed onto the slick surface of the stone. Behind the platform they were climbing was a wide, deep channel filled with water left behind by the tide.

"It smells like the cupboard under the kitchen sink," said Alex.

"Or a fishmonger's armpit," added Zoey.

They reached the highest, driest part of the platform.

"The Water Dragon is my favourite of all the stories," Anil said. "The legend says it made this cave, so I had to see it for myself. I hoped I'd find the dragon here and..."

"What?" asked Alex.

"Before I moved here, I'd hang out with my brother and cousins every weekend and we'd have these huge family dinners all the time. But my brother went to university and I never see him any more. Then we moved here, and my parents are working all the time, and I don't know anyone." Anil looked at his feet. "It's lonely, when your only friend is a seagull. If I had a *dragon* for a friend, everybody would want to know me."

"It would definitely be better company than that bird-brain," Zoey said. "I should have been more welcoming to you."

"We're sorry," Alex added.

Slowly, Anil smiled. "But now you need me."

"The only way inside the tank where they're keeping the Water Dragon is through a filtration pipe," explained Zoey. "It's underwater the whole way. We've seen people swim through it using diving gear, but we don't have any. What we do have – hopefully – is somebody who can hold their breath for a ridiculously long time."

Anil's smile grew wider. "I can hold my breath for weeks! Years!"

"So we've heard."

Finally, he grew serious. "The Water Dragon – it's really real?"

"It's real. They polluted the bay to capture the dragon. Things can't recover until the dragon is returned," said Alex. The Station had contaminated the water. But it was more than that – instinctively he knew the Water Dragon's absence would damage the ocean far beyond the bay if it lasted too long. "It needs our help."

"All right," said Anil. "Count me in."

"You're serious?" said Alex.

"No way am I missing the chance to write our own part of the legend!"

Zoey grinned. "Thank you."

The water in the channel behind the platform gurgled, ripples splashing against the rock.

"That means the tide has turned," said Anil. "We better get back."

Alex felt a twinge of panic in his chest. All at once the cavern walls seemed to press closer. The distant sound of the tide boomed loudly in his ears.

"Hurry," he said, scrambling down the rock.

"Careful or you'll—"

Alex's foot slipped out from underneath him. He tumbled sideways and splashed head first into the channel of water.

Green light flashed across his vision. Alex took a panicked breath, expecting to feel salt water sear his throat. Air flooded into his lungs instead. Words whispered in his mind. The voice of the Water Dragon, like he had heard before. Only this time he could understand it.

It spoke images directly into his consciousness.

A man cradling an egg the size of a jellyfish.

People running from the beach as a tidal wave rose behind them.

The gaping mouth of a gargantuan monster opening wide.

Hands hauled Alex out of the water. The visions and the green light vanished. Zoey and Anil stood over him.

"Are you okay?"

Alex flopped on his back, breathing hard. There was a strange tugging sensation inside him, as if some part of his body remained connected to the water, urging him to return. Almost like it had always been there, and now it was finally stirring awake.

"I was in the water." His voice was shaky. "And it didn't kill me!"

"First time for everything," said Zoey.

Alex sprang to his feet and laughed, savouring the taste of salt water on his lips. It made him feel *strong*. Like the first drink after being lost in a desert.

"I saw..." The words trailed off. The visions he had seen didn't make any sense. He only knew they had come from the Water Dragon. It was like when the creature had flicked water over him at the aquarium, the ocean helping the connection between them to grow stronger.

Disturbed by the commotion, a flurry of squeaks and chirps sounded from above them. As they peered up, the ceiling of the cavern itself seemed to flex and ripple.

"Bats," said Anil, leading the way back to the cave mouth. "Nobody realizes just how many animals rely on the ocean."

There was no sign of the sausage-less tourist by the time they walked back to the harbour.

"We'll meet again tomorrow," Alex told Anil. "We've still got more recruitment to do."

"Don't tell *anybody*," added Zoey. "Not your parents, not your cousins."

"Trust me, the last thing I want is my parents finding out. When they said I should make friends, I don't think they meant joining a crew of dragon thieves." Pinch plummeted from the sky and landed hard on his shoulder. "You know it hurts when you do that!"

They watched him stroll away towards the high street, admonishing the gull while it stared at him lovingly.

Zoey clapped her hands together. "All right, so who's next?"

Alex felt his stomach drop. The unplanned journey to the cave had taken them late into the afternoon. The visions from the Water Dragon had clouded his mind. So he had completely forgotten that today was Bridget's try-out to join the weightlifting team.

"We have to hurry!"

They set off at a run towards the gym.

CHAPTER ELEVEN

WORLD'S STRONGEST GIRL

The gym smelled of stale sweat, sour milk and broken dreams.

By the time Alex and Zoey arrived the try-out was in full swing. Overexcited parents blocked the gym entrance, forcing them to push through the crowd until they reached the front. Alex spotted Dad and Grandpa, cheering louder than anyone.

"You're late!" said Dad.

Grandpa narrowed his eyes and sniffed, as if he could smell the ocean on Alex's clothes. "And where've you two been, eh?"

Alex chose to ignore him. "Did Bridget notice?"

Dad clamped a hand on Alex's shoulder. "She told me to

tell you she'll tear your arms off later. She probably didn't mean it though."

Alex wasn't so sure.

A long bar fixed with metal plates the size of life rings sat on a wide blue mat. More plates were stacked either side. Coach Barge checked it over, ticking boxes on his clipboard. He was barrel-chested, muscular across the shoulders, with a solid mound of a belly hanging over skimpy shorts. Once he was satisfied that everything was in order he blew sharply on a whistle slung around his neck.

"After a series of back-breaking, cartilage-straining tests, only four remain to fight it out to win a place on the team! Please welcome back our remaining triallists for the final test!"

A screen had been set up at the back of the gym. Three boys in snug shorts and baggy vests draped over their muscles emerged from behind it. The third boy was a little taller than the others, longer hair knotted up in a miniature bun. He threw a wave to the coach as he passed.

"That's Baron Barge," whispered Dad. "The coach's son."

"Snot-nosed hipster clothes horse," grumbled Grandpa.

Bridget was the last to appear. She wore her bulging muscles like a fashion statement, accompanied by bright lipstick and dramatic eyeshadow, hair perfectly coiffed into a brassy sweep. Determination was etched into her face.

"It's so cool seeing your sister compete," said Zoey. "I want her to throw me around like a medicine ball."

"It's been neck-and-neck the whole way between Bridget and Baron," Dad said breathlessly as the remaining triallists lined up at the barbell.

The boys eyed the weight nervously. Bridget simply smiled and cracked her knuckles, each *pop* loud as a gunshot.

"The Olympic press is the ultimate test of any weightlifter!" announced Coach Barge. "More weight will be added until only one triallist remains."

One by one, the boys dusted their hands with white chalk and tested their grip on the thick metal bar. Next they squatted down before straightening up sharply to lift the weight onto their chest. To complete the move, they pushed the bar above their heads until their arms were locked straight, before dropping it with a heavy clatter.

Although Alex was sure his own arms would snap like sticks of rock candy, the opening weight was light enough for each boy to manage easily. The crowd cheered every successful lift.

Bridget was last to approach the bar. The crowd hushed as she dusted her hands and crouched in position.

"Blast through the burn, sweetie pie!" shouted Dad.

"Crush him under yer brawny thumb!" added Grandpa.

Bridget picked up the bar like a lunchtime baguette and hoisted it easily above her head. She flashed a smile and winked winningly before setting it back down on the mat.

More plates were added to the bar. The first boy managed to bring the weight to his chest. It stuck there while veins popped from his neck. Finally he made a noise like a flatulent seal and dropped flat onto his back. The plates thumped down either side of him, the bar driving the breath from his chest.

Coach Barge blew his whistle. "Eliminated!"

The boy was dragged limply away from the mats to make way for the remaining competitors. Both Baron and the other boy managed to lift the bar above their heads, though Alex noticed a wobble in their arms.

Bridget lifted it as if it was no heavier than before.

"I think your sister is a superhero," said Zoey. "Does she own a cape? I'm going to make her a cape."

Alex studied the barbell as even more plates were added, idly wondering how much the Water Dragon weighed in comparison.

"The weight is now increased by ten kilograms!" announced the coach.

"How much is that?" asked Alex.

Zoey considered for a moment. "Like a fat spaniel?"

The second boy chalked his hands, wrapped them tightly around the bar, and squatted down. He held the position. And held it. Gradually, the boy's face flushed red, until he had turned roughly the colour of ketchup.

"You can lift whenever you're ready," prompted the coach.

"I *am* lifting!"

There was a sharp *crack* and the boy went rigid. He let go of the bar but remained rooted to the spot.

"My back," he whimpered, the colour draining from his face altogether.

A couple of his gym mates carefully picked him up and hauled him away behind the screen.

"Just you and me," Baron said to Bridget, a quiver in his voice betraying his nerves.

Bridget smiled at him. "Soon just me."

Baron took a deep breath and chalked his hands. A wisp of powder drifted on the air as he took position over the bar.

"You've got this, son!" shouted Coach Barge.

"I thought he was supposed to be impartial," muttered Zoey.

The heavily-loaded bar drooped around Baron's hands as he heaved it up to his chest. Every centimetre of his body trembled with effort, spit flying from his mouth. For a moment it seemed he wouldn't have the strength to heft the bar any higher. Then he roared, a ferocious cry from deep in his belly, and jerked the barbell above his head.

The crowd cheered. Baron let the bar drop, making the ground tremor under their feet.

"That's my boy!" cried the coach, jumping up and down on the spot.

From behind the mat, Bridget studied the bar appraisingly. She stepped up and snapped her fingers to get the coach's attention.

"Add another ten kilograms," she said.

The crowd gasped. Coach Barge choked and almost swallowed his whistle.

"Nobody in this gym has ever lifted that much."

Bridget put a hand on her waist and popped her hip. "Not only am I going to lift it, I'm going to look fabulous doing it."

Two more plates were attached to the bar. It was completely full now. A few people in the crowd took out their phones to snap photos.

Unintimidated, Bridget crunched her neck side to side and chalked her hands. Everybody fell silent as she approached the bar, squatting down to grip the metal.

"Lift from your knees, honey!" called Dad.

Bridget took a deep breath and adjusted her feet on

the mat. The muscles in her arms and shoulders flexed as she heaved the bar off the ground. Every centimetre of her shuddered with the strain. For a moment, her knees wobbled as if they might buckle, before the bar came to rest on her chest.

Another pause. Another breath. Bridget's face flushed deep red, eyes popping.

Then she pushed the bar straight over her head in one fluid movement.

"Yes!" screamed Alex.

Even the supporters of the other contenders broke into wild cheering. Bridget, the bar still suspended over her head, threw them a wink.

"I'm going to ask your sister to marry me," said Zoey. "And I don't care about getting your blessing."

The floor shook so violently when the bar dropped that Alex was almost knocked off his feet. The crowd surged forwards to smother Bridget with congratulations. Sweat glistened on her skin. She was right – she *did* look fabulous.

Alex managed to reach her before anybody else. "That was amazing!"

"Like I don't already know that," Bridget scoffed in return.

The shrill warble of Coach Barge's whistle cut through the clamour, loud enough to get the crowd's attention.

"This competition is not over!" he bellowed, before turning to his son and pointing at the bar. "Go on, then!"

Baron's face turned the colour of sour milk. He winced at the waiting barbell, before turning back to his dad.

"I can't."

Alex grabbed his sister's wrist and threw her bulging arm into the air. The crowd began to applaud.

"Hold on just a minute!" The coach blasted his whistle again. "There appears to have been a violation!"

He marched over to snatch Bridget's hand out of the air.

"See here – nail varnish!" Bridget's nails were painted an immaculate glossy pink. "This, uh, reinforces her fingers and gives her a better grip on the bar!"

Bridget glowered at him. "That makes no sense and you know it!"

Coach Barge blew his whistle in her face. "It gives me no pleasure," he said with a broad smile on his face, "to *disqualify* you. Which means my precious firstborn son – I mean, uh, *Baron Barge* – is the winner of this try-out!"

The crowd roared in protest. Dad and Grandpa rushed the coach as if they might try and strangle him with the cord of his own whistle. Baron, the apparent winner, shifted uncomfortably from foot to foot.

Bridget seemed to deflate. She turned away from the

braying crowd and hurried off behind the screen at the back of the gym.

"I'll go after her," Alex said, leaving the others to threaten the coach with some particularly creative ideas for personal injury.

He found his sister in the cleaning cupboard that had been repurposed as the gym's female dressing room, throttling the handle of a crusty mop between her fists.

"I'm so sorry," he said.

"It doesn't matter." The wooden mop handle splintered in half.

Alex took a step back in case Bridget decided she needed something else to break. "You won. Everybody knows you were the best by a mile. I knew you were strong, but not *that* strong."

Bridget dusted the last of the chalk from her hands and dropped onto a rickety bench shoved into the corner under a shelf of cleaning sprays and suspiciously yellowed towels.

"I should have known they would never let me onto their team. I thought if I could prove I was strongest, beyond any doubt, Coach would have no choice." She sighed. "I guess I was wrong."

Alex sat down beside her. "What if there was another way?"

She narrowed her eyes at him. "I'm listening."

It felt impossible to explain about the Water Dragon without sounding as if he had lost control of his imagination. Still, Bridget listened intently while he told her everything that was happening.

"We need somebody strong enough to lift the dragon," Alex said. "And you're the strongest person I know."

Bridget thought about this for a moment. "If this is some kind of joke I *swear* I will pound your face into the ground like a fence post."

"We can't rescue the Water Dragon without you," Alex said. "My team wants to use your strength for something that really matters."

Voices echoed along the hallway outside. Baron Barge and his friends passed the cupboard in a celebratory huddle. The undeserving victor stopped in the doorway for a moment, fiddling with his hair bun.

"I'm really sorry—" he began to say, before his friends hustled him away.

Bridget clenched her fists. "All right, I'll help you. What's the worst that can happen?"

Alex decided it was probably best not to answer that question.

CHAPTER TWELVE

A SCRAPPY ENCOUNTER

Evening was settling over the bay by the time Alex and Zoey made their way along the high street towards the boatyard. Most shops had already locked up for the night.

"I'm late for dinner," said Zoey, before she stopped short and peered across to the old harbour. "Do you recognize that boat?"

A small freighter was moored at the end of the longest landing. Crewmen in black outfits threw junk onto a pile that took up most of the deck.

Alex shook his head. "It's late for your dad to have customers."

They set off at a run towards the boatyard. As they reached the gate, somebody stepped out through it. Alex bounced off them like hail against a hull and flopped to the ground.

"Sorry, I—"

The words caught in his throat when he saw who stood over him. Raze Callis smiled, holding a wrapped, square package against his chest.

"You kids should be more careful."

Alex scrambled upright. Beside him, Zoey glared at the poacher as if she could explode his head using only her mind.

Callis regarded them both with amusement. "Anybody would think you're up to no good." He pushed past them towards the harbour and the waiting boat, whistling a jaunty tune as he went.

"What was he doing here?" asked Alex.

Zoey ran across the yard towards her dad's workshop. Following behind, Alex noticed the space had been completely gutted. Usually it was cluttered with broken down motors and warped propellers, shattered masts and the occasional leaky lifeboat. Now there was nothing but scatterings of shards and splinters like early morning frost.

The only thing left was a hulking model of a sea monster cobbled together from scrap metal. Tentacles forged from stripped cables and cut tin cans trailed from the bulbous cranium of a hammerhead shark fashioned from buckled anchors. Shards of hull had been hammered flat to form a flippered serpent's tail. Mr Wu held a blazing hot welding torch against its side, showering himself with sparks.

"That man," Zoey shouted at her father. "What was he doing here?"

Mr Wu pushed up his safety visor. "You're late home again! I told you one more time and—"

Zoey cut him off. "I'm really sorry, but this is more important! What did that man buy?"

"Scrap, of course! Everything except the sea monster here for the Water Dragon ceremony tomorrow night," Mr Wu pulled a wad of banknotes from his pocket. "We really needed the money."

"You shouldn't have trusted him!"

Zoey hurried inside, reappearing moments later to fix Alex with a horrified expression. "He took Kraken!"

Alex's stomach lurched. Callis was a trophy hunter who valued beautiful animals most when they were stuffed and mounted on his wall. There was only one reason he would have taken an octopus as rare and beautiful as Kraken.

"We have to go after him," said Alex. "We have to get Kraken back."

"Hold on!" Mr Wu called after them. "You're not allowed out after dinner!"

"*I'm-eating-dinner-at-Alex's-house-okay-bye!*" Zoey shouted over her shoulder, before saying to Alex, "If Mum was here I'd be *so* grounded."

They rushed back towards the harbour. The scrap was fully loaded on the boat with a cover pulled over to hold it in place. Callis was on deck, barking orders to his crew as they prepared to sail. There was no sign of Kraken.

"We have to get on that boat," said Zoey.

"It's too dangerous."

"*You* want the stupid octopus back, and *we* need to know what Callis is planning."

"What do we do if we actually make it aboard?"

"I'll figure that out when we get there."

Without another word, Zoey scurried along the length of the jetty, taking cover behind an old wooden crate near the end. There was just enough room for Alex to squeeze in beside her, feet slipping on the seaweed that covered the rotting wooden boards. Ahead of them, the last of the crew climbed aboard the freighter, voices ringing around as they prepared to launch.

"This is a bad idea," said Alex.

Zoey nudged him. "Do you know why I believe in you? It's *because* you're always scared. You know my inventions might explode but you support me anyway, even when I've accidentally burned your eyebrows off. Again. The ocean kept trying to hurt you and there's a big bad guy with terrible sideburns but you're here anyway! You're a lot braver than you think."

The boat's rope was reeled up onto deck and the engines growled.

"I still think it's a bad idea," said Alex. "So we'd better hurry before it gets any worse."

They darted from cover and rushed towards the boat as it began to pull away from the dock. The weight of its metal cargo made it sluggish, moving carefully in the narrow spaces between the derelict fishing boats that clogged the harbour.

Zoey reached the end of the jetty and leaped. She hit the hull of the boat and caught herself on a set of rungs in the metal. Alex was slower, slipping on the seaweed underfoot. A wide gap was already opening up between him and the boat.

"Jump for it!" Zoey shouted.

The gap was too wide. Behind the boat the ocean foamed hungrily, as if slavering at the opportunity to swallow him up. If he jumped he would fall.

Except the ocean hadn't harmed him in the cave. Some secret part of him whispered that, if he fell, the water would catch him. And he couldn't leave Zoey alone and in danger. Alex kicked out into the air and flung himself forwards as hard as he could. He felt himself falling, the boat still out of reach, nothing he could do to—

A hand caught his wrist. His body slammed into the hard hull of the ship.

"Grab the ladder!"

Alex did as he was told, wrapping his fingers tightly around a cold metal rung. Zoey held onto him a moment longer as he screwed his eyes tight to avoid seeing the water churning beneath them.

"Can you climb?" she asked.

It was either climb or lose his grip and fall into the ship's propeller. Zoey led the way to the top of the ladder, where she helped Alex over the rail and onto the deck. They paused, peering around for anybody who might have spotted them. Most of the crew were busy around the scrap or posted towards the front of the boat.

"Under here." Zoey pulled up a loose flap of the cover over the scrap.

Alex ducked underneath. Enough light pushed through the cover to reveal the broken bars and twists of metal, rolls of old wiring and dented plates. A sharp barb jabbed into his back as they hunkered down together.

"You said you'd work out what to do when we got here," Alex said. "So what do we do?"

Zoey's eyes glistened in the dark. "We wait and see where he's taking us."

CHAPTER THIRTEEN
THE DRAGON CAGE

The cover over the scrap metal hid the ship's journey from them. Only when the vessel began to sway harder, buffeting side-to-side, did Alex know they must have left the bay. The wind and waves were so much fiercer on the open ocean. The thought of the wild water surrounding him on all sides made him feel sick.

"I have a number of questions," Alex whispered to Zoey.

"Shoot."

"One – why have we put ourselves in such terrible danger? Two – how are we going to get *out* of such terrible danger?"

Zoey dismissed his concerns with a wave. "We'll worry about all that when we have to."

"I'd argue strongly that we should worry about it now."

"There's no way we can let him turn Kraken into a paperweight, right?" said Zoey. "Plus we should find out why Callis – possibly the worst person alive – was looking at the aquarium blueprints and wants all this scrap metal. He's been chasing the Water Dragon for decades. Now he has it! There's no way he'll just sell it to the highest bidder."

Alex allowed himself a moment to consider her argument. "Are these real worries or are you making excuses for being so reckless?"

"Probably a little of both."

"As long as I'm allowed to freak out a bit about being on a boat."

"I'll allow it."

The ship lurched over a wave. Alex braced himself as his stomach performed a seasick backflip. Just a few hours earlier he had fallen into the water and survived. Maybe the ocean wasn't his enemy any more. Maybe he no longer needed to be afraid.

"Are you okay?" asked Zoey.

He swallowed and nodded. "I think so."

Finally, the pitch of the engine shifted and the boat began to slow. Voices called from somewhere distant, growing closer as the boat manoeuvred towards its destination. A jolting bump told them they had stopped.

Footsteps hurried past on deck, centimetres from their

hiding place. Alex held his breath until he was sure they had passed.

Light flashed on the outside of the cover. Zoey lifted the edge to peer outside. "It's the lighthouse – we really are a long way out! We're mooring up beside an even bigger ship. It's got a hatch in the deck. I think they're going to push the scrap into it."

"We're going to get caught."

"Not necessarily." Zoey studied the pile of junk metal looming over them. "We can hide in there."

A small tin boat was tangled upside down in a knot of old cables. Together they wormed inside, lying with their stomachs across the wooden benches to hold themselves safely under the boat's shell.

"I suppose it's pointless to ask if you have a plan," said Alex.

"I have a *sort of* plan," Zoey replied blithely. "It would work better if this boat had seat belts."

A dreadful grumble reverberated through the metal, its clangour moving through the scrap like a pulse. The wires and cables around them hummed in harmonious response.

"It sounds like we're going to be eaten alive."

The growl grew louder and louder, like a lion losing patience with its trainer. Fragments of scrap rained down on the outside of their hiding place with deafening crashes. Underneath them, the deck detached and began to lift up, tipping at an angle.

"Hold on tight!" shouted Zoey.

The angle grew steeper, and steeper, until all at once the scrap began to slide. It tumbled away from the smaller ship and clattered through the hatch of the larger one. Their tin boat flipped as it fell, and they clung to the benches as it dropped into the belly of the other ship.

A mound of scrap waited inside. The tin boat landed with a jarring crunch. Its hull was slick enough that it slipped, spilling off the edge of the heap and surfing down its side to send them clear of the heavy junk that continued to pour in from above.

The boat skidded to a halt.

"That was the most dangerous thing I've ever done," said Zoey. "I think I kind of loved it?"

Alex felt as if his bones had been rattled into dust. He climbed out of the tin boat and was relieved to find all his limbs still attached to his body. Zoey was stuck under the benches, so it was only once he'd prised her loose that he noticed where they had ended up.

The air was stiflingly hot. Every breath burned his throat. High bulkheads on all sides showed the scale of the ship they had been thrown inside. A staircase took them up for a better view. At the top was a catwalk around the outer edge of the space.

Heat wavering on the air made it hard to understand what Alex was seeing. The scrap was being poured into a square pit of liquid fire. It melted instantly into lava, flaring orange and red to throw strange shadows from the blackened machinery around the pit.

"That could have been us," said Alex.

"Why does Callis need a whole foundry?" Zoey said. "I wish *I* had a whole foundry."

It was clear the scrap metal was being melted down so it could be turned into something new. But what?

A heavy door groaned open a little further along the gantry. Alex and Zoey ducked away behind a crate.

Raze Callis stepped out to look over the foundry below. A group of crew followed him, including one dressed in full safety gear, a heavy visor pushed up onto her forehead to reveal frightened eyes.

"No more excuses," shouted Callis. "You're the chief engineer and I've supplied you with all the metal you need!"

"Captain, it's not just about the materials," replied the engineer with a trembling voice. "We're building as fast as we can in the circumstances but—"

Callis turned on her. "If it isn't ready by tomorrow night, we lose our chance."

"I understand, captain." The engineer sagged. "We'll work through the night."

Callis studied her through narrowed eyes for a moment. Then he nodded back the way they had come. "Show me your progress."

Keeping a safe distance, Alex and Zoey followed them through the door.

Across a corridor and through another hatch brought them into an even larger space. A platform overlooked a wide pool closed inside the belly of the ship. A thick chain trailed from the ceiling to plunge down into the water.

Callis and crew crossed to the railing, leaving enough space behind them for Alex and Zoey to creep into the shadow of the bulkhead. The air here was far cooler – the sweat on their skin quickly chilled and made them shiver.

"Bring it up!" called the engineer.

A machine whirred. The chain rattled as it was reeled up like a gigantic fishing line. A large, rectangular shape emerged from the pool: a cage attached to the end of the chain like a gigantic crab trap, its sides forged from thick metal bars. As it turned on its chain, Alex saw that the far side of the cage was empty, open, no bars yet fitted into the frame.

Callis barked a triumphant laugh. "Truly, it's the biggest cage I've ever seen."

He turned back to his crew, a wicked smile breaking across his face.

"Big enough even to hold a dragon."

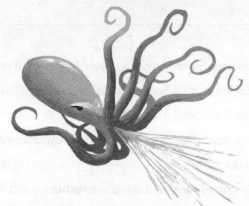

CHAPTER FOURTEEN

DRAGON HUNTING RUNS IN THE BLOOD

Callis was going to steal the Water Dragon for himself. After years of searching for it, he wanted finally to claim its powers. Everything he had told the mayor was a lie.

"Of course he wouldn't just help Parch sell it. You were right," whispered Alex, looking at the unfinished cage in horror. "Sort of."

"I sort of often am," Zoey replied.

The engineer was still talking rapidly about her unfinished accomplishment. "From my understanding of the dragon's current size, sir, your request to enlarge the cage seems unnecessary to—"

Callis cut her off. "The beast is in its most diminished state. Removing it from the ocean forces it to shrink so that it might conserve power and survive. Once it returns to its natural habitat we will need every inch of that cage."

While Callis continued to pepper the engineer with further demands, Zoey tugged on Alex's arm and pointed to another door a little further along the platform. They snuck across while the crew's attention was on the cage. The door led into a narrow passageway. The air smelled dank. Puddles splashed under their feet as they hurried through the ship.

"Now aren't you glad we came here?" said Zoey. "We've found *another* evil plot we need to stop."

"Yeah, I'm thrilled."

The passageway turned a sharp corner and the air grew fresher. "We need to know how he's planning to make his move."

"And get my octopus back," said Alex.

"And find out exactly what he's planning to do with the Water Dragon."

"And get my octopus back."

"Yes and get your stupid octopus back!"

At the end of the passage was a spiral staircase leading upwards. They paused at the top, hearing a couple of crew members pass in the corridor beyond, then tiptoed out. Doors led to various rooms: a bar with a sea shanty playing through fuzzy speakers, a couple of crew gripping bottles and laughing uproariously; a shower room where somebody was singing tunelessly in one of the cubicles.

"Look," said Alex, a tarnished sign screwed into the wall catching his eye.

Captain's Quarters.

An arrow pointed up another flight of stairs. At the top was an ornate wooden door of varnished wood. It didn't budge when Alex shoved it. Zoey threw a kick but only succeeded in hurting her foot.

"If this is Callis's office, we need to get inside!" said Alex.

There was a noise on the other side of the door. The handle rattled and moments later the lock *clicked.* Alex and Zoey jumped away as the door swung inward.

A bright blue octopus greeted them on the other side.

"Kraken!"

Alex ran to scoop her up. The octopus wrapped her arms tightly around his wrist and hugged close.

Stepping into the office was like entering a nightmare. Alongside the expected desk, plush leather chair, and globe-shaped drinks cabinet, the walls were decorated with grisly animal trophies. Bleached shark jaws were displayed behind the desk. The mounted heads of sawfish, narwhals and sea lions stared blankly down at them from every direction. A rack of harpoon guns was displayed in a glass case, the points polished to a wicked shine. Beside a laptop on the desk rested a bright red, snub-nosed pistol.

These animals had been killed for nothing more than bragging rights. Alex had to fight the urge to smash every trophy into pieces.

"Cool, a flare gun!" said Zoey, lunging for the red pistol.

"Please don't pick up the dangerous firearm."

"Fine." Zoey reached for the laptop instead. "Let's see what we can find."

The screen lit up. A series of internet tabs showed reports on man-made disasters from all over the world. The first showed an oil spill in the Mexican gulf, the usually sparkling blue water stained black. Seabirds huddled on rocks, feathers covered in sludge. Others showed a massive island of rubbish somewhere in the middle of the ocean, swathes of bleached coral on the Great Barrier Reef.

Zoey started clicking at random until she found a scan of the aquarium blueprints and a satellite image of the bay with notes added to it. "Look! He's not going to steal the dragon from the aquarium. He's going to wait until the buyer transports it out of there and then snatch it. That's so...lazy!"

Alex was distracted by a painted portrait tucked between trophies on the wall. Faded colours depicted a man with greasy hair spilling from beneath a wide-brimmed hat and a mouth missing half its teeth. One foot was propped on a cannon, a harpoon gripped in his hands. Alex recognized him immediately – it was the same image they sold on postcards in the shop.

"It's Brineblood," he said.

Zoey shot up from the desk to study the portrait. "Look," she said.

A small brass plate on the bottom of the frame bore a simple inscription:

CLARENCE CALLIS
1768

The real name of the pirate from the story, who had hunted the Water Dragon and died trying to capture it in the bay.

"Raze Callis and Brineblood are *related*," Alex said.

"Raze must be his great-great-great-*great*-grandson."

Voices approached the cabin door. Callis, barking orders to his crew.

"We're trapped," Alex hissed.

Zoey slammed the laptop shut and picked up the flare gun. "We have to run for it."

"Run where? We're on a ship in the middle of the ocean."

"We'll work that out when—"

"I shouldn't have asked." Alex positioned himself by the door, gripping the handle in his sweaty hands. Kraken climbed up on his shoulder. The voices were right outside.

"Three, two, one..." Zoey aimed the flare gun at the door. *"Now!"*

Alex threw the door open. The hulking form of Callis blocked the other side, already raising a harpoon gun. Before he or Zoey could open fire, Kraken sprang into action. The octopus's skin shifted to bright red as she arched her body and fired a bullet of water. It hit Callis between the eyes, making him stumble backwards and drop the harpoon.

"Go!" shouted Zoey, shoving the flare gun into her pocket.

They bundled out of the room and sprinted past Callis. Two more crew members came running towards the noise but Kraken dispatched them with expertly placed shots.

"This way!"

A hatch led out onto the deck. They were somewhere in the middle of the ship, the prow and the stern stretching away to either side.

"Let's go to starboard!" said Zoey.

"Which way is that?"

"Um, left, I think?"

An alarm began to ring behind them, an electronic whooping that resounded through the entire ship.

"Let's just be anywhere but here."

The lighthouse overhead swept light across the deck. Every time it passed they hurried towards the back of the ship. One crew member who tried to intercept them hit the deck with a blast of salty water to the eyes, while another was knocked off balance and tumbled over the railing into the sea below.

Finally, they reached the stern of the ship. Zoey reached out to pet Kraken's head. "I take back anything bad I ever said about you."

The beam from the lighthouse was temporarily blinding before it winked away. The stout cylinder was perched on a cluster of jagged rocks. Other boats were moored around it, almost invisible until the light passed over.

Callis was hiding an entire fleet behind the lighthouse.

"That explains why Mayor Parch fired the lighthouse keeper," said Zoey. "Callis wanted him out of the way."

"We have to go before they're all after us."

A ladder took them down to a docking platform close to the water. The ocean was a dark expanse stretching ahead of them. In the distance a smudge of light showed where Haven Bay was waiting for them to return.

"You're not going to like the next part of my plan," said Zoey.

"It's really not a plan if you're making it up as you go along."

"I think we have no choice but to swim for it."

Alex felt his legs turn to jelly at the thought. He had gone swimming in a pool a handful of times but never in open water. "It's too far away. We'll never make it."

The alarm continued to blare. Voices shouted back and forth across the ship. Footsteps thumped along the deck as the crew worked to hunt them down. It was only a matter of time before they were caught.

Before him, the ocean beckoned to Alex. The Water Dragon's voice echoed in his mind, imploring him to trust the water. It hadn't harmed him in the caves. Instead he had felt connected to the ocean, as if a long-dormant part of himself was struggling to awaken. If he had faith in the water, if he could fully open himself to it, he was sure it would save them.

"Hold my hand," said Alex, kneeling at the edge. "Don't let me go."

As soon as Zoey clutched his hand, Alex took a bracing breath and plunged into the ocean.

The water closed over his head and green light flashed across his eyes. He forced himself to breathe, trusting that he wouldn't be allowed to drown.

Visions – memories sent to him by the Water Dragon – flooded through his mind, sharper than he had seen them before. Alex was inside them, as if he had gone back in time to take part.

A group of people were gathered in a cave. They all wore necklaces of seashells, their hair crunchy with salt. In front of him stood a broad, bare-chested man, necklace missing from his throat. He cradled a jelly-like egg, a sac that sagged over his arms. A dark shape squirmed inside. Others pushed past Alex, shouting in dismay, trying to reach the egg.

Forbidden, *Alex understood.* Stolen.

More men kept the protesters away, throwing them to the ground and brandishing swords.

Alex reached for the egg but the scene changed abruptly around him. There was sand underneath his feet. Wind lashed at his skin as a storm raged overhead. People were fleeing along the beach. Alex turned to the water and saw a tidal wave rearing up, careening directly for them. He cried out and began to run, knowing there was no hope of escape.

The roar of the wave was deafening. Moments before it reached them, Alex tripped and sprawled in the sand. A colossus was rising from the ocean. The wave broke around it, tremendous spines trailing from its chin. It was the Water Dragon, blown up to a hundred times the size. Its fierce eyes caught the sun and flashed like lighthouse lanterns. The horizon disappeared behind its monumental head, despite

most of its body remaining submerged. Up the dragon
loomed, and up, a thick column of scales and spines.
This was the Water Dragon at full size, before it was
poisoned and plucked from the ocean.

Titanic jaws opened wide to blot the sun. Alex
screamed as teeth crunched down—

The story of Haven Bay's creation was true. But now he knew what the people who lived here had done to the Water Dragon to cause it: they had stolen its egg.

Although the visions had ended, Alex still felt the dragon's presence. The water connected them.

"I'll do whatever I can to help you," he told it in his mind. "I want to make it right."

The green glow around him intensified. Alex gasped as a torrent of power swelled from somewhere deep inside him – power he realized had always been there, hidden and weakened by his fear of the ocean but never extinguished.

Now the Water Dragon had awakened it, and the power *surged.*

Alex reached out his hand. Delicate vortexes weaved through the water towards him, each infinitely long, threading away to the unknown ends of the ocean. He felt how the threads connected to millions of living creatures all over the world. They tied him to distant reefs and atolls, to shallow harbours and deepest abyss.

Calling for help just meant tugging on the right thread.

A handmade wave lifted him deftly back onto the docking platform. The alarm still blared behind him.

"What just happened?" asked Zoey.

Guards appeared at the rail above them, shouting for others to join them.

Alex smiled. "I can get us out of here."

He dipped a hand and reached again for the threads of the ocean. One pluck brought a wave rolling up to slam into the hull of the ship. It tipped sideways fiercely enough to send the crew trying to reach them floundering overboard.

Two dark blurs appeared on the waves, heading rapidly towards them. Fins cut through the surf.

"Sharks!" screamed Zoey.

"Not quite."

The sweeping beam of the lighthouse revealed a pair of dolphins pulling up beside the docking platform, clicking urgently. Alex lifted his hands to stroke their slick backs and long noses.

"Meet our getaway drivers."

First he helped Zoey into the water so she could lie along the length of a dolphin's back and cling to its fin.

Then he made sure Kraken was secure on his shoulder, reached for the other dolphin, and held on tight as they were whisked away from the boat towards the distant lights of the bay.

CHAPTER FIFTEEN

THE FINAL RECRUIT

A splash of cold water wrenched Alex from dream-troubled sleep. All night he had dreamed of losing his grip on the dolphin fin, waves boiling up to pull him under a smothering blanket of darkness.

Except, every time it happened, his power swelled and he took control of the ocean. It became part of his body and carried him to safety.

Alex swiped the water from his eyes to find Grandpa standing over him with an empty glass.

"Wakey-wakey!"

"What was that for?" Alex moaned, sitting up sharply.

Grandpa grabbed the end of the bed covers and whipped them away. "Why are there sea otters in yer bed?"

The otters had cuddled up around his neck for the night and still slumbered there like a hairy scarf. Apparently they were tired after spending the previous day devouring the food Alex had left and making a mess of the room in his absence.

"It's a long story," said Alex.

"I suppose nothin' should surprise me no more." Grandpa hurled clothes at him. "Get dressed and let's go. You're with me on the van today."

The ice cream van was waiting outside. It was only mid morning but the high street was already busy, stalls and booths opening early for the Water Dragon ceremony that night. They climbed into the van and set off along the sea wall.

"Where'd yer get to last night?" asked Grandpa.

"Hanging out with Zoey." Alex didn't like lying to Grandpa. But *technically* he was telling the truth.

They parked close to the beach. Instead of opening the serving window, Grandpa got out of the van.

"Aren't we selling ice cream?" asked Alex.

"Not until we've had a little chat."

On the beach, the tide was halfway up the breakwater. Grandpa began climbing to the top of the stacked stones, forcing Alex to follow.

The sheen of oil on the water's surface was bright in the

morning sun. They reached the end of the breakwater and Alex gazed out towards the mouth of the bay. Hidden behind the lighthouse, Callis's fleet lurked. If they were to have any chance of saving the Water Dragon, they had to break it free before the poacher could claim it for his own.

"I knew I couldn't keep yer out of the water for ever," said Grandpa.

Alex watched him closely. "What do you mean?"

"I was on the beach last night when you and Zoey washed up on dolphin-back. You tellin' me that's how you spend all yer time together?"

The only way to escape the conversation would be to fling himself into the filthy water and swim for it. Instead, Alex decided it was time to tell the truth, however unlikely it might sound.

"The Water Dragon is real. A poacher has captured it. We have to break it free. Tonight, actually."

Alex took a deep breath and spilled everything that had happened in the last few days. When he'd finished it felt like a sandbag had been lifted off his chest.

"So this Raze Callis has been usin' the mayor to finish what his ancestor started!" concluded Grandpa.

Alex blinked. "You believe me?"

"Of course I believe you! Yer grandma always told me it were all true. The ocean is so vast we don't know half of what calls it home. Don't stop us doing our level best to kill it all stone dead anyways."

"What did Grandma know about it?" asked Alex. "She was just as scared of the ocean as me."

"You might say she had a love-hate sort of relationship with the sea." Grandpa sighed. "It's time yer knew how I met yer grandma... When I was a young man, I'd take a rowin' boat out every night and go swimming." Grandpa fixed his eyes on the horizon. "In summer, the bay was warm as a fresh drawn bath and in winter cold enough to freeze yer cockles off."

Alex shivered at the thought.

"One summer evenin' I fell fast asleep in the boat," continued Grandpa. "By the time I woke up it were almost dark. The current had carried me clean out into open water. The town was so far off it looked like the bay had a mouthful of stars. I started rowin' back, fast as I could, but out there the ocean is wild. It smashed my boat against the rocks and punched a hole clean through. I had no choice but to swim for it."

It was hard to imagine Grandpa having the energy to swim. A single flight of stairs made him huff and puff like a lone oarsman rowing a warship.

"Just when I were ready to give up and let the ocean take me, she appeared." Grandpa sighed wistfully. "The most beautiful woman my eyes ever clapped upon, as if she had risen up from the depths themselves."

"A mermaid?" asked Alex.

Grandpa chuckled. "I thought the very same. She took my hand and helped bring me back to shore. She gave me the strength I needed to make it home."

"So where did she come from?" Alex asked.

"She told me she were one of those people what lived 'ere hundreds of years ago," Grandpa replied, mouth twisting into a smile, as if he could hardly believe what he was saying. "Before the bay were even formed."

Alex wanted to laugh. It sounded so ridiculous! Except until just a few days ago he had thought the Water Dragon was nothing but a fairy tale.

"They stole the dragon's egg," Alex said, remembering the vision the Water Dragon had shown him. "That's why it turned against them."

"Before that the dragon had given 'em power well beyond a normal human – they could breathe underwater and chat with the fish. Long life an' all! Everythin' they needed to live in harmony with the ocean. But a few of 'em craved more." Grandpa shook his head. "They envied how the dragon could control the waves, whip up a storm and command the sea animals. They decided to take the power for themselves. If *they* had authority over the ocean, they could rule over everythin' and everybody. So they stole the egg before anybody else – including yer grandma – could stop 'em."

Alex swallowed down his anger. "What happened to the egg?"

"Lost when the dragon attacked." Grandpa's voice hitched in his throat. "Only yer grandma and a handful of her people survived and escaped. Hundreds of years she spent trying to find the egg, trying to find a way to put right the wrong her people did the Water Dragon. But it was always after her, driven mad by grief, wantin' revenge against any of 'em what survived. By the time yer grandma found me she thought the egg must have been destroyed. She was so tired of running. Her only choice was to find somewhere to hide where it couldn't reach her. A haven. So she gave up the sea for good and swore to live only on land for the rest of her days."

A tear rolled down Grandpa's cheek. Alex took his hand and squeezed it tight.

"After she came ashore, all the powers the dragon had given her dried up. She started to age just like the rest of us," Grandpa said. "Never went near the water again. It were the only way to stop the dragon huntin' her."

"You said she wasn't the only one who survived the attack, so did the dragon hunt the others too?" said Alex.

"All the others went into hiding. Yer grandma was the only one out there tryin' to put it right."

"Couldn't the dragon just lay another egg?"

Grandpa shook his head. "There used to be more than one Water Dragon, y'see – just enough to keep all the oceans of the world safe and balanced. There couldn't be too many of 'em or everythin' would be knocked out of whack. So each one was born with a single egg inside it."

"The other Water Dragons…" Alex trailed off, scared that he already knew the answer.

"They disappeared over time. Hunted or overwhelmed by everythin' we've done to the sea."

The Water Dragon – *his* Water Dragon – was the only one left. It had to single-handedly try and protect the ocean from the damage and pollution inflicted by the world. No wonder it had been angry enough to spend centuries hunting Grandma down. Angry enough to send the sea after her grandson too.

Grandpa gripped Alex's shoulders tight and looked into his eyes. "It was always clear yer took after her, even though yer dad and sister don't. That's why we had to keep yer out the water. Because of somethin' her people did hundreds of years ago."

Alex could hardly speak. Being able to hear the Water Dragon's voice, speaking to the animals, strumming the chords of the ocean. He had inherited it all from Grandma. The one person who had tried to make sure he would never know.

"You should have told me," he said.

"We thought it were safer to keep it hidden," said Grandpa. "Easier to keep yer out the water."

"It was never the ocean itself that tried to hurt me." Alex remembered the threads of the ocean at his fingertips, how it all connected. "The Water Dragon knew when I went into the sea and sent it to attack me. But it's different now. I have to rescue the Water Dragon. I can put right what Grandma never could."

Grandpa shook his head. "It's too dangerous."

"It's way more dangerous if we do nothing! What happens to the oceans if there's no dragon left to protect them?"

Alex knew Grandpa cared about the sea, but he cared more about his grandson's safety. If Alex could *show* him that the dragon and the water were no longer a threat...

He climbed down to the base of the breakwater where waves lapped against rock. Before Grandpa could stop him, he slipped into the sea.

"Get out of there right now!" Grandpa bellowed.

Alex ignored him. A thread of ocean tickled his fingers. It danced away when he snatched for it, flexing just out of reach. The power was an essential piece of him, like an extra organ, but he still needed to learn how to use it.

Gently, he opened his palm and beckoned the thread towards him. It settled into his palm like a dog resting its chin. Alex took hold and *heaved*.

Flexing his new-found power felt like a tidal wave coursing through every muscle in his body. It ached. The thread was *heavy*. He thought of Bridget's workouts – he would need to exercise his powers to easily wield them. To discover how strong they could be.

Alex gritted his teeth and kept pulling the thread. The water beside the bank of rocks bubbled. A dark shape rose from underneath, growing larger as it approached the surface.

"What is it?" asked Grandpa, bracing himself as if for a blow.

The wreck of a rowing boat breached alongside the breakwater. Algae and seaweed coated a broken wooden hull, speckled with limpets like sub-aquatic stars. Water poured from inside as the wreck saw daylight for the first time in decades.

"That's my boat. From the night she saved me," said Grandpa quietly. "You're doing this?"

Alex nodded. Holding up the wreck took every scrap of his concentration. He could only keep it there for a moment before the effort was too much. The sunken vessel gulped and glugged as it returned to the depths.

"You're more like her than I knew," said Grandpa.

"I don't think I'm exactly the same. But I think maybe there was always a small piece of her sleeping inside me," Alex said, breathing hard. "The Water Dragon woke it up so I can help it protect the ocean."

Grandpa reached out a hand. Alex took it and climbed back onto the rocks.

"All right," said Grandpa. "But only if I can help."

"It's going to be dangerous."

"Even more reason yer need me! Anyway, how exactly did yer think you were going to get a whoppin' great dragon all the way from the aquarium to the bay?"

"We're going to use sliding mats to—"

Grandpa waved the idea away like a bothersome fly. "That's a terrible plan. We'll use the ice cream van."

Alex felt a smile creep across his face. "You really want to help us?"

"Of course I do! I've been tryin' to keep you safe yer whole life. No reason I should stop now."

They pulled each other into a tight hug, the tide sluicing through the rocks under their feet.

The growl of an engine behind them shattered the moment, swiftly growing louder. A speedboat entered the bay, skipping over the waves like a stone hurled by a giant. Following behind was a horde of mismatched vessels. Pleasure yachts were flanked by jet skis, elaborate sailing boats gliding alongside roaring hovercraft. Together they raced into the bay like tourists fighting to claim the best sunbathing spot on the beach.

Thundering past them, the armada's turbulence stirred up the waves and sent spray cascading over the rocks.

"The auction is tonight!" Alex shouted over the din of engines. "These must be the bidders."

By the time they were back at the harbour every available berth was occupied by a luxury boat. Some of the larger yachts had anchored out on the water.

"I guess the only thing Callis wasn't lying about was how many people would want the Water Dragon."

The new arrivals swarmed the high street. Men in flashy suits and expensive sunglasses gathered in groups, blocking the pavement. The locals eyed them warily, keeping their distance. A woman with a fox skin wrapped around her neck screeched her sports car to a halt to ask Mrs Bilge for directions.

"I know your type!" the old woman blustered. "You keep your hands off our town!"

Cannonball launched a volley of wheezy barks at the car as it sped away.

"Even the dog knows these are rotten people," said Grandpa.

Alex clenched his fists. "We've got a plan. Time to put it into action."

CHAPTER SIXTEEN

OCEAN'S FIVE

The inflatable paddling pool was just deep enough for Anil to duck under the surface and hold there for as long as his lungs could stand.

"How long was that?" he gasped after emerging once again.

Alex read the time from Grandpa's old stopwatch. "One minute and ten seconds."

Anil slapped the water in frustration, spraying Alex and the watching otters. "I can hold my breath for longer. I *know* I can."

Their entire team had gathered in Mr Wu's boatyard and spent the day practising every step of the plan. There was no time to change it now. Evening was falling and soon they would need to set off for the aquarium.

It had taken a lengthy combination of explaining, pleading and nagging for Zoey to convince her dad to let her take part in the plan. Like Grandpa, he insisted on helping make sure it was as safe as possible and set about customizing the ice cream van to accommodate a dragon.

The contents of the van were now spilled across the yard, as if it had eaten too much of its own product and thrown up. Cans of drink were stacked haphazardly against the side of the office, joined by metal shelves and cupboard doors. The ice cream machine itself was lying on the gravel, dripping melted vanilla onto the stones.

Zoey had welded together two enormous chest freezers that usually stored ice creams and lollies into a single massive unit. She had insisted on doing it herself, forcing her dad to supervise. When it was finished he inspected the work at great length before giving his approval. Zoey tried to hide her smile, but Alex caught it as she unwound a hose to pump water into the new container.

Zoey's dad towed over his model sea monster for the ceremony – which Alex reckoned was about the same size as the real thing – so they could check the fit.

"It looks amazing, Mr Wu."

He beamed. "I can't wait for the whole town to see what I can really do."

Grandpa studied the double-wide fridge. "Tight fit for a dragon. But we only need to cram it in there for a few minutes while we get it down to the bay."

"If everything goes to plan," said Alex.

Grandpa scratched his bald head. "Aye."

"Okay, everybody gather around!" bellowed Zoey. "We know Callis isn't making his move until after the auction. That gives us a window *before* the auction kicks off. By the time anybody finds out the dragon is gone it'll be too late for Callis to catch us."

"Speaking of getting caught, did my parents call?" asked Anil.

Grandpa nodded. "I told 'em yer stayin' the night with Alex. Technically I wasn't lyin', and they were too happy about yer havin' some pals to ask questions."

"Tonight, we're not friends," said Zoey. "We're dragon thieves."

She wiped clean the price-list whiteboard on the outside of the ice cream van. Kraken perched haughtily on Zoey's shoulder and waved her arms as if conducting the briefing. "We'll split into three teams and use code names in case they're listening to our radio chatter." She scribbled on the whiteboard. "Bridget will be Striking Sturgeon, Alex will be Beluga Puke, and—"

"Can I please be anything but that?" Alex interrupted.

"I'm afraid the code names are firmly set in stone."

"And what's yours?"

"You will all be referring to me throughout the operation as Awesome Angelfish."

"I definitely won't be," Alex muttered.

Zoey drew a roughly circular blob on the whiteboard. Kraken lifted an arm to point into its centre.

"Striking Sturgeon, Beluga Puke, and Tunnel Turtle – that's you, Anil – will infiltrate the park through the front entrance. I have acquired the necessary disguises." Zoey held up the mayor's coat she had stolen from his office. "Though we're still relying on Alex's new-found, uh, *powers* to make this work."

Alex turned to the group of otters and cleared his throat. They had listened to him once before. Now his powers had properly awakened, surely they would again.

"Attention!" he barked.

The otters stared up at him dumbly and didn't budge.

Alex sighed. Although the power was part of him, he couldn't force it. It was a privilege given to him by the Water Dragon. So before he tried again he closed his eyes and held the image of the dragon in his mind. The ocean and its creatures weren't for him to command. His power made them his allies in the fight to keep the oceans safe.

"Would you kindly assume stack formation, please?"

Alex said calmly. A wave of power moved through him, like it did when he reached for a thread of the sea.

Clumsily, the otters fumbled into a furry pile, climbing one on top of the other until they formed a swaying tower.

"Now walk?" suggested Alex.

The otters stumbled forwards, immediately lost their balance, and fell into a bristly heap at his feet.

"We both need a bit more practice."

Zoey sighed. "The infiltration teams will use the decoy to get them inside, and then to draw the attention of the guests so they can safely reach the Water Dragon." She scribbled a smiling lizard onto the whiteboard. "That's when Tunnel Turtle will take the harness through the filtration pipe."

"And once he's got the dragon hooked up, I'll lift it out of the tank," said Bridget. "Piece of cake."

As soon as they freed the Water Dragon from the tank they would break a panel in the outer glass wall of the aquarium. The ice cream van would be waiting. Then all they had to do was load the dragon inside and get out of there before anybody realized the main attraction of the night had been stolen.

"I'll be watching everything from above."

With a flourish, Zoey revealed the drone she had been working on for so long. A large metal shell like an insect's carapace extended out on either side into four flat propellers the size of dinner plates. A doll's head had been bolted, upside down, onto its belly.

"There's a camera in the head," she said proudly.

"That is the most horrifying thing I've ever seen," said Alex.

Mr Wu was watching closely. "Does it actually fly?"

"I worked really hard to get it right," said Zoey, picking up a radio controller. One button press made the propellers whir to life. Her fingers swept across the controls and the contraption heaved itself up to hover choppily on the air.

"It's..." Mr Wu watched open-mouthed. "...beautiful."

When the drone landed, Mr Wu hurried inside and returned with a paint palette and brush. In a few smooth strokes, he painted Chinese characters onto the drone's shell.

加油

"What does it say?" asked Alex.

"Literally, it means to add oil. But it's more than that – it's an expression of support, to cheer people on."

Zoey and her dad both wiped grease from their foreheads and smiled at each other.

Finally, the time came for them to finish loading the van and set off for the park. Kraken and the otters plopped into the freezer and Zoey distributed an assortment of black clothes and mismatched flat caps.

"If nobody looks too hard they'll pass for real guard uniforms," she said. Lastly, she handed Alex the mayor's coat. "Hopefully they'll all be looking at this instead."

When everybody was dressed they turned to Alex, as if they needed his approval to continue. Nervously, he cleared his throat.

"This is going to be really difficult. It's probably the stupidest thing any of us has ever done."

"I think you're supposed to be inspiring us," said Zoey.

"But we're doing it anyway, because it's the right thing to do," Alex continued. "True strength is standing up for what you believe in, even when it would be easier not to."

"Also dead-lifting a postbox," added Bridget.

"We believe in what makes this town special," Alex went on. "We believe in the importance of looking after the bay, and the ocean, and everything that calls it home. Like we call Haven Bay home. So...let's go and do the right thing."

He looked between them anxiously, expecting them to laugh at him or change their minds about the whole idea. Instead they smiled and nodded, patting his shoulder as they filed past him to climb into the van. Grandpa got behind the wheel, while Mr Wu hugged his daughter before heading over to open the boatyard gate.

"Good speech," said Zoey.

"Thanks."

"I hope it isn't the last speech I ever hear."

Alex climbed into the van beside her. "Me too."

CHAPTER SEVENTEEN

FUNNY LOOKING MAYOR
YOU GOT THERE

The length of the driveway leading to the aquarium was jammed with expensive cars, lights flashing and horns honking as chauffeurs jostled for the closest parking spots. The people they had seen arrive by yacht streamed towards the aquarium entrance. The sun was setting fast, a full moon rising up to replace it. In town, the Water Dragon ceremony would be in full swing, everybody too distracted to notice what was happening at the top of the hill.

Alex, Zoey and Anil held on tight in the back of the ice cream van as the wheels bumbled over the uneven road. Kraken and the otters gripped the side of the repurposed freezer as the cold water splashed around, sloshing over the sides to soak the group's freshly polished black shoes.

"How come she gets the front seat?" called Alex.

Bridget peered around the headrest and smirked. "Because *she* can break you in half with her little finger."

Grandpa steered them onto the grass and stopped as close to the aquarium as they could get. Guards posted at the entrance kept their attention on the guests streaming inside.

"I got walkie-talkies so we can communicate," said Zoey, presenting Alex with an orange plastic handset that looked like an old children's toy. "It's the best I could find."

Alex held it close to his ear. "Do they work?"

"Testing – Awesome Angelfish to Beluga Puke?" Zoey said into her identical walkie-talkie.

"I hear you loud and—"

"TESTING!" Zoey bellowed, making his ears ring.

Grandpa switched off the engine. The guards had spotted the van and were eyeing it suspiciously.

"Everybody ready?" he said.

Alex looked between them all dressed in their hastily cobbled together black uniforms. The odds were so stacked against them that it seemed ridiculous to even try.

He closed his eyes and felt the tug of the nearby Water Dragon, as if they were connected by one of the watery threads of the ocean even here. Power seemed to reverberate along it, building in rippling waves of potential, as if getting closer to the dragon made Alex stronger. It filled him with confidence. There was no way he would turn back now.

"We're ready," he said.

Grandpa reached up and flicked a switch on the roof of the van. The chimes began to play a jangling song that rang out into the night. "Hurry it up. It won't be long before they realize I've got nothin' to serve."

Unable to resist the lure of ice cream, some of the guests peeled away from the crowd to approach the van. Grandpa slid open the serving window to greet a man wearing a bowler hat and glasses slung on a chain around his neck.

"Do you have any sorbet? I'd like to cleanse my palate before sampling the canapés. You know how it is!"

"Can you change a fifty-pound note?" asked the woman behind him.

The forming queue provided enough of a distraction for Alex to safely open the back doors. They climbed out onto the grass and quickly gathered the bags containing their equipment.

"I'll send up the drone," said Zoey.

The rotors whirred as she launched the machine into the air. It hovered for a moment, the eyes of the doll's head winking at them, before Zoey sent it darting upwards into the night sky. An image on her phone flickered. At first it showed nothing but splotches of light like underwater phosphorescence. Gradually it stabilized to show an aerial view of the aquarium through the grubby glass roof of the building.

"I won't be able to see everything," she said. Alex thought she almost sounded nervous.

"We'll just have to be extra careful," he said.

Lastly, he summoned the otters out of the van and asked them to kindly stack up. Bridget approached them with the mayor's coat.

"You think this is going to work?"

Alex shrugged. "I'm pretty sure none of the guests have actually met the mayor before."

Bridget slung the coat around the otters, fastening it at the front so they were completely hidden underneath the plush material. She added a chunky fake golden chain that hung loosely around where the neck was supposed to be. The otters trilled and fidgeted impatiently under their disguise.

Next, Alex reached inside the jacket of his uniform and took out Kraken. The octopus was placed on top of the otter stack and a wide, feathered hat positioned on her head.

"Camouflage," said Alex.

The blue of Kraken's skin faded to a sallow pink, darker spots remaining to approximate eyes, nose and mouth. She could almost pass for a human face under the shadow cast by the brim of the hat.

"It looks weird," said Bridget.

"Yeah, but so does Mayor Parch."

"Fair point. Let's go."

The makeshift mayor shuffled forwards, robe dragging along the ground. Alex, Anil and Bridget followed close behind, scanning the crowd for threats like real bodyguards.

"Turn right," whispered Alex.

The robe meant Alex had to guide the otters the best he could. Kraken, with two arms outstretched to create shoulders and the rest tucked away in the collar, tried to steer the stack.

Some of the guards had run off to join the increasingly impatient queue extending from the ice cream van. Those remaining stood to attention and let them straight through when they saw what they thought was the mayor approaching.

"So far so good," said Alex. "Just keep moving."

The otters tottered forwards, almost losing their balance, before standing straight again and shuffling through the gate.

"Are you okay, Your Lordship?" asked one of the guards.

Bridget grabbed a sleeve of the coat and used it to wave

the concern away, at the same time stepping across to block the guard's view.

The walkie-talkie crackled in Alex's pocket, Zoey's fuzzy voice pushing quietly through the speaker. "All the guests are still on Oceanic Avenue."

Every tank on the boulevard had been polished until it shone. The water inside was sparkling clean, the black iron frames scrubbed of rust and cobwebs. Even the tank ornaments had been washed, the serpent's head flashing sharp stone teeth, the bronze diving helmet gleaming. The guests milled around on the pathway picking morsels of food from silver trays carried by waiting staff in bow ties.

"I see little kebabs, salmon rolls, what looks like grilled—" came Zoey's voice from his pocket.

"You can study the menu *after* we haven't been caught."

The baroque double doors through to the dragon tank were closed, a red velvet rope slung across to keep people away until the auction began. Several eager guests already waited outside.

"We have to get them away from the doors so we can get through to the dragon," whispered Alex. "It's time to draw some attention."

The makeshift mayor lurched sideways and pirouetted on the spot before catching its balance. It was enough to make people spot it and hurry over to fawn and flatter.

"Lord Mayor!" called a woman wearing a sleek black dress and diamond necklace. "You're looking...*interesting* this evening."

"I just wanted to say that these canapés are *delightful!*" said a man with a white jumper tied around his shoulders, holding a half-eaten crab puff. "I wondered if I could trouble you for the name of your chef? I'd love to have them on my next fishing expedition."

More people – including those who had been blocking the doors – gathered to hear the answer. One of the otters let out a sharp squawk from underneath the robe.

"What was that, old boy?" said the man. "You haven't tried them? Oh, you must!"

He pushed the rest of the crab puff towards Kraken underneath the hat. The octopus reached out a suckered arm to snatch it away, making the man stumble back in alarm.

"Let's go," said Alex.

They hurried towards the freshly cleared archway. Before opening the doors, Alex quickly scanned around for anybody watching. He caught sight of Callis standing in the shadows between two tanks. The poacher narrowed his eyes at the imposter mayor now holding court with half the guests.

At the same moment, a great burst of fanfare sounded

from the front gates. A guard in sharp black uniform stepped into the crowd and cleared his throat to make an announcement.

"Introducing Lord Mayor of Haven Bay, patron of this auction, the only reason you're all here tonight... the honourable, actually-an-average-height-if-you-look-at-statistics, Humbertus Parch!"

The real mayor stepped through the gates. Dressed in full ceremonial robes, golden chain clanking around his neck, he waved regally at the bemused crowd.

The mayor's grand entrance was distraction enough for Alex to open the doors and wave Anil and Bridget through. While the guests looked away, the otters evacuated the coat, dropping to the ground and scurrying away to hide, taking Kraken with them.

By the time Callis and anybody else turned back there was nothing to see but an empty coat and golden chain lying on the ground.

Alex quickly shut the door behind him. They had reached the tank.

Now they just needed to get the Water Dragon out of it before the auction started.

CHAPTER EIGHTEEN

THE LOWEST BIDDERS

The Water Dragon unfurled its sinuous body to greet them. It was waiting close to the side of the tank, as if it had anticipated their arrival. It tapped its chin spines against the glass, milky eyes settling on Alex as he approached.

The fresh understanding between them had transformed his fear of the creature into something closer to awe. Now Alex saw how countless colours eddied deep within the dragon's scales, smothered by the leaden grey that dulled their surface. He sensed the strength in every coil and sinew of its length, the power lying dormant within, doused by poison and pollution.

"We're going to get you out," he said.

That hidden, ancient power would flourish as soon as

they returned the Water Dragon to the ocean. It would be *free*.

"O-M-G," said Bridget. "It's *actually* a dragon."

Anil punched the air. "I knew it was real!"

There was no time for them to gawk. A small stage with a microphone had been erected in front of the tank. Two columns of empty chairs faced it, ready for the guests once the auction began. It wouldn't be long before they streamed through the archway.

"Anil, are you ready?"

By the time Alex turned around Anil had already stripped down to his skimpy swimming trunks. Bridget averted her eyes as she tied a rope securely around his waist. It was long enough that they could keep hold of one end while Anil entered the tank. They pulled the cover off the filtration pipe and helped him climb onto the edge. Water gurgled and slurped around his legs.

"If you get into trouble, tug the rope twice," Bridget told him.

Anil flashed her a winning grin. "Don't you worry about me."

He took a single deep breath and ducked into the pipe. The rope began to run through their hands as he pulled himself up into the water-filled tunnel that ran around the side of the tank.

Alex spoke into the walkie-talkie. "Anil is inside the filtration pipe."

"You mean Tunnel Turtle?" replied Zoey.

"You know exactly who I mean."

Keeping a tight hold on the lifeline, Alex pressed a hand against the cool glass of the tank. The Water Dragon drifted close on the other side. When Alex closed his eyes and listened, it was no longer currents of despair and anger he heard. It was the gentle tide of hope.

"Heads up! We've got a problem." Zoey's voice was urgent. "Two guards heading straight for you!"

Alex and Bridget scrambled out of sight just in time to hide themselves from a pair of guards wandering lazily towards the tank. The rope still trailed into the mouth of the pipe.

"Do fish have souls?" asked the first guard.

"I hope not," replied the second. "Or this place must be full of fish ghosts."

Alex was really glad that Zoey couldn't hear the conversation.

The guards kept their distance from the tank, stopping on the far side of the path to peer at the Water Dragon.

"You think it's real?" asked the first guard.

"Nah, I reckon it's computer graphics or something." Still, neither of them dared to move any closer.

The safety rope stopped feeding through Alex and Bridget's hands. Inside the pipe, Anil must have realized the guards were there and waited. If he emerged inside the tank now the guards would spot him immediately.

"We need to pull him out," whispered Bridget.

"Just wait." Alex realized his knuckles were turning white where he tightly gripped the rope.

The guards continued to linger.

"You heard what this lot are willing to pay?" said the first guard, jerking a thumb over his shoulder at the archway, where the guests were gathering on the other side of the doors.

The second guard whistled low and long. "A pretty penny for some fancy fish fingers."

The first guard caught sight of the rope and took a step towards it. Alex held his breath. Inside the tank, the Water Dragon opened its mouth in a bubbling roar, showing off the sharpness of its teeth. The guards squeaked in fright and hurried back to the party on the other side of the doors.

Bubbles rushed into the tank as soon as they were gone. Anil burst from the pipe inside and kicked powerfully to the surface. He sucked hungrily at the air, ignoring the dragon drifting beneath him.

Alex hurried out from their hiding place. "Are you okay?"

Anil gasped another breath before breaking into a

wide smile. "New record! I can't wait to tell my brother!"

He steadied himself against the side of the tank and began reeling the rope in through the filtration tunnel.

Anil peered down at the dragon. "It's definitely *not* going to eat me, right?"

"I didn't bring you here to be a snack."

Old fishing nets had been sewn into the middle of the rope to create a harness that would support the Water Dragon's weight. Anil ducked underwater to tuck it around the dragon's armour-plated middle, before looping the rope and tying a knot to hold it in place. Then he hurled the trailing end over the side of the tank for Bridget to catch.

"Heck." The walkie-talkie fizzed. "We have a problem," said Zoey.

"I'm really getting sick of you saying that."

"Then I just won't tell you that the guests are moving towards the doors for the auction to start."

Alex snapped his head around to look. The doors began to push open. But before they were wider than a crack, Mayor Parch stepped across to block the way.

"Ladies and gentlemen, it is my utmost pleasure and a tremendous honour to welcome you all to our humble seaside town on such a beautiful evening!"

He stopped as if waiting for applause. Nobody gave him any.

"We have to hurry!" said Alex.

Bridget wrapped the rope around her wrist and planted her feet wide on the path. "Let's hope I'm as strong as I think I am."

She heaved on the rope. Her arms flexed and the muscles in her back rippled. Immediately the Water Dragon was lifted to the top of the water. It let out a low rumble that made the glass vibrate.

"It's okay," Alex whispered, sure the creature could understand him. "We're trying to help."

The dragon would have to bear the indignity of being winched tortuously slowly from the tank. Bridget's face burned bright red as she strained on the rope. The dragon grew heavier as soon as it was clear of the water. Alex found a space beside his sister and added his meagre strength to the effort. Anil tried to push from underneath.

"You need to get out of there!" Alex shouted to him.

Anil strained underneath the dragon. "I can help!"

"Quickly!" urged Zoey from the walkie-talkie. Alex pictured her in the back of the ice cream van, watching helplessly.

Thankfully, the mayor would never pass up an opportunity to deliver a long-winded speech to a captive audience. "As a boy I dreamed of discovering something truly special, something no eyes had ever gazed upon before.

Finally, my dream has become reality."

"And now you're going to sell it," muttered Alex.

The Water Dragon was approaching the top of the tank, wriggling uncomfortably as its writhing body sagged over the harness tied around its middle. Alex thought its weight might pull his arms straight out of their sockets.

On the other side of the doors, Mayor Parch cleared his throat. "Tonight I present you all with a truly once in a lifetime opportunity. You may have read about such a creature in fairy tales and old pirate stories, but *never* has such a thing been captured alive. Until now! I will prove to you all that the myths are true."

A murmur of excitement – or perhaps impatience – rippled through the audience.

The shoulders of Bridget's T-shirt ripped open as she heaved the Water Dragon to the top of the tank. It swayed and swivelled against the edge, one last tug required to tip it over.

"I'm beginning to think catching it with our bare hands wasn't such a brilliant idea," said Alex as the dragon loomed over them. Its head trailed over the lip of the tank, long-suffering eyes watching them closely.

"Exactly none of this was a brilliant idea," Bridget replied through gritted teeth. "No other choice now!"

Beyond the doorway, the mayor was turning the final

corner of his speech. "So without further ado, allow me to introduce you to our auction's first and only lot. A magnificent creature! A singularly rare and exceptional phenomenon! A tremendous investment!"

"Hurry!" shouted Zoey in Alex's ear.

Alex and Bridget tugged on the rope as hard as they could. The dragon's body began to roll over the edge of the tank.

It was too late. The doors were thrown open with a dramatic flourish.

Every set of eyes landed on the Water Dragon suspended awkwardly in the air above the tank on a rope, and the pair of sweating, terrified children that held it there.

CHAPTER NINETEEN

KEEP YOUR ARMS INSIDE
THE RIDE AT ALL TIMES

The Water Dragon hooked its head over the side of the tank and pulled itself forwards. Alex and Bridget gave the rope a final jerk and the dragon wriggled over the lip of the glass. It rolled in the air as it fell, turning its armoured back to break the fall. There was no choice but to throw out their arms and catch it.

It was like trying to catch a cannonball. The weight of the dragon knocked them off their feet and left them pinned underneath it.

"Seize them!" bellowed Mayor Parch.

"I'm not sure," said Zoey through the walkie-talkie, "but I think you've been rumbled."

Everybody seemed to snap into action at once. The

guests surged backwards in terror, jamming shoulder-to-shoulder in the archway and blocking the guards behind them.

It was the only chance they would get to escape, but Alex was completely trapped by the Water Dragon. Even Bridget, heaving with all her might, couldn't get it off them.

Guards managed to push through to the front of the crowd. The sight of the dragon loose from its tank was enough to make them advance with caution.

A rumbling started deep inside the Water Dragon's body, a seismic groan like tectonic plates shifting deep under the seabed. It grew into a resonant quaking, as if the dragon's scales were vibrating together in terrible concert.

Alex felt his skin begin to tingle. Closing his eyes, he felt the dragon's power lash against him. It was weak, but it reverberated along the invisible thread that connected them, teasing out the power inside him, drawing on it to charge up its own. It made his whole body hum with giddy energy.

"Get ready," he said, flexing his fingers.

Beyond the archway, the tanks lining the thoroughfare began to vibrate. The water inside stirred and sloshed against the glass.

Behind the crowd he spotted Callis, looking on calmly amid the commotion. The poacher was the first to notice the waves sloshing inside the tanks. Their frames creaked as water strained against them. Cracks spidered through the glass. Iron popped and snapped. The crowd turned to watch the water beat mercilessly against its prisons.

The membrane around the Water Dragon's neck puffed full. The trickle of power inside Alex became a torrent.

Every tank ruptured at the same moment. But instead of raging along the avenue, the water picked itself up into living shapes, liquid legs tottering onto the path. The figures carried the tank ornaments with them: the shape of a man lumbered forward with a brass diving bell for a head, spears of rock strengthening its aqueous arms as it lunged at the guests. Tendrils of weed flailed around a stone serpent's head, the water supporting it plaited into a slithering snake's body. A shark with blazing gems for eyes and the broken hull of a model battleship for a fin snapped its watery jaws.

The liquid army advanced on the crowd from all sides. A few people tried to fight back, swinging canes and bejewelled handbags, but they splashed harmlessly through the bodies.

"I can't swim!" trilled a woman as the serpent swallowed her whole, leaving her to peer out from inside its transparent body.

"This suit is cashmere!" complained a man as the shark chomped wetly on his legs.

Mayor Parch cowered as a figure with a treasure chest for a head, the lid flapping like a gaping mouth, lurched over him.

"Help me!"

The mayor's guards dodged the stampeding crowd to run towards the dragon.

Amid the chaos, Alex saw Callis study the scene, before slipping away out of sight.

"We're still trapped!" said Bridget.

Alex laid a hand flat on the Water Dragon's scaly hide and let its power wash through him once more. It connected him to the ocean – to the currents that surged through it, the pressure of the pitch-black bottomless deep, waves crashing against shore. Together they had the strength to wield it all.

The water inside the giant tank beside them lifted itself up into a heaving swell and slammed against the glass.

"Whoa!" shouted Anil, still afloat inside.

Imprisonment away from the ocean had kept the Water Dragon separated from its full power. The new bond between the dragon and Alex amplified it, like lightning snapping at storm-tossed waves.

Another wave smashed against the side of the tank hard enough to make it collapse. A miniature ocean rushed after it as a surging wall. The watery figures collapsed into the wave. The guards made a final run towards them but were swept off their feet.

The wave held together and reared up like a living creature. Alex felt the dragon's power threading through it, wrapping a protective bubble around him, Bridget and Anil. The irrepressible deluge picked up the Water Dragon and washed them all towards the back of the aquarium.

The force of the water broke open the glass outer wall. They held tight to the dragon's armour plates as the torrent carried them careening down the slope beyond. Water wrapped around them, cushioning them against the bumps and dips in the hill, leaving a pocket of air so they could breathe. The waterfall bore them whipping past bushes and scrub in the darkness.

"The water will protect us!" Alex shouted. "Trust it and we'll be okay!"

Night had fallen while they were in the aquarium and the lights of the houses on the street below briskly drew closer, blurring across his vision as they reached top speed. After several more tumultuous seconds the slope began to level out before it reached the road. The wave held firm and tall, letting them all sink through it to rest safely on the ground, before the power dissipated and the water washed away across the tarmac.

"That was *amazing*!" Anil said. "Can I go again?"

Bridget patted over the Water Dragon. "Is it okay?"

The dragon's body heaved with laboured breaths, but the wave and its hardened scales had protected it from injury. It lay unravelled at the edge of the road like a gigantic over-cooked noodle, its power spent. Alex knew how much it was relying on them now.

A dog barked on the pavement behind them. In the light of the full moon overhead, they found Mrs Bilge rooted to the spot, Cannonball hiding behind her trembling legs.

Alex picked up the sodden rope. "We're just taking our new dog for a walk."

Mrs Bilge's voice quivered. "What breed is he?"

"Um...aquatic?"

Bridget patted the Water Dragon's mighty head. "Good boy."

With a huff, Mrs Bilge hurried past, tugging Cannonball after her before the dog ended up as a midnight snack.

"What do we do now?" asked Bridget as soon as the old lady was gone. "We can't drag it all the way to the ocean."

They were so close! Only a few streets lay between them and the refuge of the bay. But it was enough to leave them stranded.

A cacophony of bells like wind chimes clanging in a tornado sounded from the end of the street. Wheels squealed to accompany it.

The ice cream van skidded around the corner, chimes playing at full blast. It screeched to a halt in front of them. Grandpa shut off the engine and Zoey jumped out of the cab. She raised a hand to catch her drone as it dropped out of the sky.

"Need a lift?" she said.

CHAPTER TWENTY

DRAGON WAGON

Together they heaved the Water Dragon off the road. Bridget led the way, hooking her thick arms around its equally thick neck, shuffling to the ice cream van and lifting it into the back. Displaced water poured from the double-wide freezer. The others followed to try and tuck its wide tail fin inside.

The dragon was far too large for the container. Its tail trailed out of the back door and its head was pushed against the windscreen. Only its middle sagged into the water. When it met Alex's eye it looked distinctly unimpressed. A huffed breath fogged the front glass.

Alex reached forwards to lay a hand on its rough nose. The Water Dragon lifted its head as if to nuzzle at the touch.

The connection between them flexed and green light smouldered in its scales.

"We need to hit the road," said Grandpa, clambering into the driver's seat. "If we found you, Callis won't be far behind."

They crammed themselves around the dragon. Alex couldn't help but laugh. They had actually done it! It may not have gone exactly to plan, but nevertheless they had rescued the Water Dragon. All they had to do was return it to the ocean and they had won. When he caught Zoey's eye she grinned broadly back at him.

Grandpa drove gently down the hill towards the seafront. A discarded paper cup rolled against Alex's foot. He picked it up and used it to pour water over the dragon's head and tail. Wind rushed through the van from the open back doors.

"I'll get as close to the water as I can manage," said Grandpa.

"Then we lift it straight into the bay," added Bridget, giving Alex a meaningful look. "No delays."

Alex nodded. Although it had only been a few days, he would miss the Water Dragon. He trailed his fingers in the water and allowed himself to relish the tingle of energy that seemed to flow between them.

The van glided past Mr Wu's boatyard to reach the

harbour. Grandpa manoeuvred to reverse along the widest jetty, wheels skidding on the slippery seaweed that covered its planks.

The sea appeared as a flat, black sheet. The high sides of the smaller boats and pleasure crafts moored along the jetties by the auction guests blocked their view of the town. Whenever the lighthouse beam swept around, it pushed sharp shafts of light through the gaps between them.

Open, the back doors faced the water. Everybody gathered around the dragon to take their share of its weight. Before they could begin to lift, Alex spotted movement in the shadows between boats.

"We don't have all day!" said Bridget.

Alex strained his eyes against the darkness of the bay. "Something isn't right."

The grumble of an engine rolled across the water. The inky night made it impossible to pinpoint where it came from. Zoey appeared at his shoulder.

"What the heck is it?" she asked.

Alex lowered himself to lie flat on the damp boards of the jetty and stretched an arm over the side. He could reach just far enough to trail his fingertips in the water. He squeezed his eyes shut and listened to what the bay could tell him.

Multiple shadows moving across the water. Lights hidden.

Boats.

Brought into the bay from behind the lighthouse to lie in wait.

Alex pulled his hand away and shot to his feet. "It's a trap! They're waiting for us to release the Water Dragon so they can capture it for themselves!"

All at once the bay seemed to catch fire. Lights flared up across the water, one by one, revealing a fleet surrounding the boatyard. Every boat they had seen hiding behind the lighthouse. A spotlight fixed on the van, its glare forcing them to shield their eyes.

"We have to go!" shouted Alex.

Grandpa revved the engine to life. Their headlights lit up the jetty. People emerged from the shadows to cut off their escape. The last to step into the light was the hulking figure of Raze Callis, harpoon gun resting against his shoulder, a triumphant smile breaking across his face.

CHAPTER TWENTY-ONE

SEAWEED SMACKDOWN

No amount of threatening revving would intimidate Callis and his crew into making way for the ice cream van.

"I have to say I'm impressed. I didn't think you'd actually pull it off," called Callis. He took a step closer to the van. "That mayor of yours is even more incompetent than I'd reckoned."

Alex walked around to the front of the van, glad that Zoey, Anil and Bridget went with him. "Mayor Parch hired you. You're supposed to be working for him."

"That's what the most honourable lord bonehead believes," said Callis. "I needed him to let me build the Station so I could pump enough toxin into the water. I've been chasing that there beastie my whole life! My ancestor

– *Brineblood*, you people call him – had the right idea. Why keep haring around the world when he could trap it somewhere it loves? The same place *he* loved before that dragon destroyed it."

Alex's heart jolted inside his chest. "Brineblood was one of the ancient people who lived here?"

Callis barked a laugh. "It was my ancestor who stole the egg! Imagine hatching your own Water Dragon, raising and taming it to use its power in whatever way you tell it. He could have ruled the world."

Behind him, the Water Dragon gave a fluting, anguished cry. It had heard every word of Callis's story.

"If he had the egg, why did he need to go after the dragon?"

"He lost it!" Callis snarled. "The egg was never seen again after his home was destroyed. So he had no choice but to go after the dragon itself. Now I'm going to finish what he started."

It was clear that Callis didn't understand the dragon's power. It was a raw, elemental force that could never be tamed. Not by him, and not by Alex.

"You're no different to Brineblood," Alex spat. "You're making the same mistakes."

"My only mistake was trusting the idiots in this wretched little town!" Callis called back. "The promise of an auction and a big payday got your mayor onside. Everything was going to plan until that buffoon decided to stash the dragon in an aquarium on top of a hill instead of inside the Station like I told him. As you know, it doesn't make for an easy heist. So why not let whichever fool coughed up the most cash go to the trouble of getting it out of there before I take it for myself? At least that way I pocket the money too."

Alex clenched his fists. "We got there before you."

Callis barked out a laugh that skipped across the water. "You think you can go around asking for blueprints and sneak onto *my* ship without me doing some investigating of my own? I got wind of your little plan. I figured on the off chance you succeeded, I could steal the beast from you just the same as anybody else. I suppose I should thank you for doing all the hard work." The smile fell from his face. "Now hand it over without any trouble and I'll let you all go. That's only fair."

Alex wanted to scream. They had come so far. They were *right* beside the bay. They couldn't give up now.

"It'll die if it doesn't return to the water," he said. "It has to keep the oceans safe!"

Callis shifted the harpoon gun from one shoulder to the other. "I've spent my whole life on the waves. I don't want the beast as another trophy or as the star attraction in some amusement park. Only I know what it can really do.

I want to harness its powers to put a stop to disasters all over the world."

"You're lying."

"Oil spills! Ice caps melting! Coral reefs bleaching and dying! That beast has the power to fix any of them! I have the resources to take it where it's needed most and make sure every scrap of damage is made right."

Alex looked to the others gathered around him. While they remained steely-faced, he could sense uncertainty creeping up on them.

"You promise you want to help?"

"Of course!" Callis eyed the Water Dragon hungrily. "Assuming people pay me enough, of course."

Alex felt his blood run cold. "You're going to *rent* the Water Dragon out to fix the damage people are doing to the ocean?"

"People will pay a pretty penny to make sure they don't have to actually make any changes to how they live," Callis growled. "The beast can give them that."

Anger boiled through Alex's veins. "And anybody who can't afford to pay just has to watch the ocean die around them and suffer the consequences?"

Callis smiled. "That's just the way of the world, kid."

"It doesn't have to be."

Casually, Callis lifted the harpoon gun from his shoulder

and lightly tested his finger against its barbed tip.

"I've hunted the most dangerous creatures this planet has to offer. You see this scar?" He touched the point of the harpoon to the damaged skin on his arm. "I pulled a shark over twenty-foot long out of the deep. It broke loose on deck. Tore the skin and muscle away like lasagne. It still ended up on my wall with all the rest." Callis lifted his eyes to meet Alex's hard stare. "Your beast there is out of power after that stunt at the park. You really think you stand a chance against me without it?"

Alex felt his legs shake underneath him. A shark would only attack like that if it was cornered and desperate. Fighting for its life.

Exactly like they were now.

He turned to the others gathered around him. "Get back into the van."

All three ignored him, stubbornly standing their ground.

"Trust me," Alex told them. "You're going to want to get out of the way."

Grudgingly, they shuffled backwards around the ice cream van and climbed inside the back doors.

"The Water Dragon isn't the only one with power," Alex said, turning back to face Callis.

Having the dragon at his back filled him with confidence. He lowered himself to his knees and flattened a hand against the seaweed that covered the jetty. Salt water welled between his fingers. Alex felt for the threads and this time found them easily. The dragon whispered encouragement in the back of his mind.

For Grandma, he thought.

The seaweed twitched under his hand. A long rope of it peeled away from the rotten wooden boards and slithered along the jetty. It lashed around the ankle of one of Callis's crew and snatched him off his feet.

Tendrils of seaweed swished behind them, wrapping around chests and binding arms. Callis swung the harpoon to defend himself, slashing cords of the assailing weed, but a thick strand hooked around his ankle and lifted him into the air. As he dangled upside down there his eyes fixed on Alex in disbelief.

"It wasn't just the dragon. It was *you*. You're like me," Callis said. "But…how can you wield our ancestors' powers when I never could?"

"I'm nothing like you." Alex clambered into the van. "Grandpa! Go!"

"We're goin' to have to talk about these powers of yours." Grandpa reached up and set the chimes playing like a battle cry. "Hold on tight!"

The engine roared. The van shot towards the captive crew. The rushing headlights flared in Callis's eyes. At the last moment, the seaweed hurled him and his henchmen flailing into the dirty water.

"He won't let us get away so easy," said Grandpa.

Alex looked past the dragon's tail trailing from the open back doors and saw Callis already climbing out of the water.

"They don't know this place like we do," said Zoey. "There must be somewhere we can hide."

"The cave!" said Anil. "There's no way they could find us inside the old dragon tunnels."

There didn't seem to be any other choice. "We have to get 'em off our tail first," said Grandpa.

As the van reached the edge of town, an engine roared on the road behind. Through the back doors, Alex saw Callis's four-by-four rapidly gaining on them.

"We need to go faster!"

"An ice cream van is designed to be chased by children," Grandpa called back. "This is top speed!"

Headlights blinded them as the filthy four-by-four growled close. One of his crew was behind the wheel, freeing a dripping Callis to lean out of the side window and aim his harpoon gun directly at them.

They turned onto the high street. Cobbles made the van bounce and sway. The brakes screeched as Grandpa brought them to a sudden halt.

"What are you—?"

The high street was packed with people. Strings of lights and stalls selling hot snacks lined the road.

"It's the Water Dragon ceremony!" said Zoey.

Alex had been so preoccupied with the rescue that he had completely forgotten.

Most of the gathered crowd were locals. Everybody turned to look at the ice cream van nudging its way along the street, the Water Dragon's tail trailing from the back doors.

"Look at that!" shouted Mr Ballister.

"I don't believe it!" cried Mrs Bilge.

Alex held his breath and waited for the uproar. The dragon was *real*. Instead, everybody began to cheer, the crowd opening up to let the van pass.

"It's the best model yet!"

"So realistic!"

Anil laughed. "They think it's the model sea monster for the Brineblood chase!"

"Dad is going to be so disappointed," said Zoey.

The crowd closed up again around the back of the van, cutting off Callis's four-by-four. Alex threw the poacher a wave as he was forced to pull back.

One by one, the locals lifted up their Brineblood scarecrows and paraded them behind the ice cream van and the dragon trailing from it. Together they launched into the traditional ceremonial song.

"Old Brineblood sought to snag the sea
and crush it under heel.
He chased the monster, made it flee
and trapped it with his zeal!"

Everybody sang along at the tops of their voices, lifting their effigies in time with the rhythm, banging the beat on the sides of the van.

"The monster sheltered in the bay,
a haven of its own.
Rousing its powers for the fray
it gobbled Brineblood's wicked bones!"

As they picked up speed, the procession turned into a chase. The song broke off as everybody ran after the van, hollering excitedly.

Traditionally, the ceremony ended with the model sea monster being taken to the beach so it could escape the evil clutches of the Brineblood mob into the bay. Instead, Grandpa steered up the hill towards the cliffs. The crowd came to a confused stop, blocking Callis into the high street.

The town fell away behind them. The Water Dragon lifted its head from the front passenger seat, nostrils flaring as if it could smell the closeness of the ocean. Alex lay a hand on its hard scales. They were so close to freedom, yet still so far.

As the land began to rise into the cliffs, they reached the broken headland. The collapsing church brewed in the darkness.

"Pull off here," instructed Anil.

A swampy verge sloped down from the road towards the old graveyard that surrounded the church. Half the plots had tumbled into the sea, headstones and monuments overhanging the drop below.

"How do we get into the cave from up here?" asked Zoey.

"A tunnel comes out somewhere." Anil tramped across the mud, scanning the graves, searching for a specific name. Many were old enough that the engravings had worn away. Moss blanketed the stones, the ground dipping where coffins had rotted and given way underneath.

Anil stopped in front of a gravestone fallen flat on the ground. Alex read the faded inscription.

CLARENCE CALLIS

1736–1770

LOST AT SEA

He couldn't help but laugh.

"Brineblood's empty grave. That has to be a sign," said Zoey. "Not sure if it's good or bad though."

Bridget was tasked with moving the gravestone away.

"You're paying for my next manicure," she grumbled.

A steep tunnel plunged down into the ground, far deeper than a grave, as pitch black inside as if it had been painted there. Anil peered into its depths uncertainly.

"There's a problem."

Alex sighed. "I feel like I've heard that a lot tonight."

Anil pointed into the mouth of the tunnel. "The tide is high."

Although it was impossible to see far into the tunnel, the sound of the sea gurgling somewhere below was clear for them all to hear. The rising tide was filling up the cliffs from inside.

"I've never been in this part at high tide. It'll be rough – underwater most of the way," said Anil. "It leads to the cavern I showed you before. We'll be safe there, but it's a long swim."

Alex stumbled back. "I can't."

Zoey caught him by the shoulders. "I thought you weren't scared any more?"

Discovering the Water Dragon and the truth of Grandma's life had done so much to erode his fear of the ocean. Still, the thought of being swallowed, lost deep inside an underwater tunnel with no way out, made him want to run from the bay and never return.

Headlights flashed on the road behind them. Callis must have escaped the ceremony and resumed the chase. It wouldn't take him long to track them down.

"I'll use the van to draw him off," said Grandpa. "You have to go fast."

They unloaded the Water Dragon as gently as they could. The mouth of the tunnel was just wide enough for it to fit inside.

"Hide in the caves. He won't find yer there," said Grandpa, climbing back into the driver's seat. "If yer try and get the dragon away now his men will catch you. In the mornin' we can see exactly what we're up against." He held Alex's eye. "You can do this. Look at everythin' you've done already."

Engine grumbling and chimes ringing loud across the cliff top, the van pulled back onto the road and sped away into the darkness. The other headlights were gaining fast.

Anil sat and dangled his legs into the hole. "I'll lead the way. Bring the dragon behind me. And don't get lost. You might never get out again."

The tunnel was steep enough that as soon as he climbed

inside he slid quickly out of sight. A few seconds later they heard the splash of him landing in the water below.

Bridget brought the Water Dragon to the mouth of the tunnel. Alex reached out to stroke its head. Its power was weak now, only a trickle, but Alex knew it could grow into a roaring river. That same strength could help him to do this.

"You'll be right behind us," said Bridget.

A rumble like a roll of thunder resounded inside the dragon as Bridget pushed it into the tunnel. She grabbed hold of its tail and let it pull her into the fall. The splash seconds later was so much louder.

Alex stared down into the hole. "I'm scared."

"The water doesn't want to hurt you any more. The dragon has proved that," said Zoey. "You were scared about everything we had to do tonight. You did it anyway. You're the bravest person I know."

"What about you?"

"*Obviously* I'm super brave too." She took his hand and he felt how it trembled. Behind them, the headlights had grown bright and close on the road, illuminating the broken walls of the church. "We go together, okay?"

They stepped to the brink of Brineblood's grave. Its darkness lapped hungrily at their toes.

"Jump on the count of three," Zoey said.

"Okay."

"One—" Zoey counted, before she decided not to waste any more time and tipped them both headlong over the edge and down.

CHAPTER TWENTY-TWO

DARKNESS

Alex thought they would slide down the ravenous throat of the cliffs for ever. Loose soil and coarse rock scraped his skin as they picked up speed, skidding full tilt along the steep tunnel, darkness rising up to swallow them. He held tight to Zoey's hand. Nothing bad could happen if they stayed together. No matter what, he wouldn't let go.

The tunnel abruptly came to an end and the ground dropped out from underneath them. There was a moment of free fall before the water hit him like concrete. Pain quaked through his body as the impact forced the air from his lungs. It would have been too much to bear if the cold hadn't cloaked him in numbness almost immediately. Alex desperately wanted to breathe. He fought the ache nagging in his chest, pushed at the water with both hands to—

Both hands.

Zoey wasn't there.

He spun around underwater but the darkness was crushingly absolute. Alex was alone in the water.

Desperately, he kicked his frozen legs. His head broke the surface and he gasped at the chill, rank air. The roar of crashing waves drummed against his ears and straight away he was whisked up, grazing against a rough stone wall it was too dark to see.

The tide was pouring into the cave, narrow tunnels channelling the water into fierce streams that spewed out here, smashing and rolling as they rushed to fill the space. The noise clamoured deafeningly around the cavern.

"Zoey?" Alex shouted, trying to lift his voice above the racket.

Another wave pulled him under. The water seemed bottomless, an abyss yawning beneath his feet.

When he broke the surface again, he thought he caught a snatch of Zoey's voice.

"— have to swim for it!"

Her words were devoured by the constant roaring that filled the cave. They would never be able to find each other in the stormy darkness. Alex fought to control his breathing and smother his rising panic. He reached for the threads of the ocean, sure he could calm the water if he pulled on the right one. But his terror amid the tumult made them impossible to grasp, the threads whipping out of reach as soon as he touched them.

The water knocked him against the wall, stone cold and slick against his skin. If he stayed here much longer he would be dashed against the rock and drowned. There was no choice but to carry on alone. He just had to hope that Zoey had done the same.

Except there was no way to tell how to escape the cave. Alex ran his hands along the wall, searching for an opening. Somewhere close by he could feel water tugging at him as if trying to draw him towards it, a slurping sound rising through the rest of the noise. Waves tried to prise him loose as he fumbled desperately along the wall. Finally his hands found a break in the stone, water rushing to fill whatever space lay on the other side.

Alex just managed to snatch a breath before he was dragged through the hole. Rough stone pinched close on either side. A tunnel, brimming with cold and darkness, threatening to suffocate him. It was impossible to tell if his eyes were open or closed.

The current slowed. It no longer pulled Alex along. The tunnel must have filled to the top, no room left for more water to flow inside.

Keep moving. That's what Anil had said. The only way he would make it was to push on into the black.

Alex kicked blindly forwards, the water growing colder as he fumbled deeper into the tunnel. His lungs began to ache. The blackout disorientated him. What if he wasn't going forwards at all? He flung out an arm, hoping Zoey would be there to take it and guide him to safety, but instead he only grazed his knuckles on unrelenting stone.

If he could stay calm, master his panic, his new-found power would let him breathe underwater. It would keep him safe. But his heart was beating so rapidly that he couldn't concentrate, couldn't remember how to bring the power to the surface.

Now his lungs screamed for air. He *had* to breathe. Automatically his body lifted itself up, searching for the surface. The top of his head collided with solid rock.

Maybe there was still time to turn back. He might not have gone too far. Except he could no longer tell which way was forward and which way back.

Light flashed across his eyes. The first sign of his body giving in to the water?

Scales brushed past him in the darkness. A long, lithe shape glowing green nosed at him urgently.

As soon as Alex touched the Water Dragon the parched ache in his chest subsided and he fell into another memory...

The dragon cut powerfully through the ocean, hearing the countless voices of everything that lived under its surface. The fatigue of a long voyage far from home throbbed the entire length of its body.

A burrow on the sea floor opened into a den constructed from compacted mud, shells and driftwood. In the centre was a nest of rocks and weed. It nudged the cover aside to find—

Nothing.

The nest was empty.

It bellowed, shocked at the roar of pain and fury that erupted from deep inside it. The egg it had nurtured for so long was gone.

And beside the nest, dropped carelessly into the mud, a necklace of shells strung together by human hand.

It howled with rage and surged from its den, smashing the walls apart, rushing towards the coast to destroy them all.

The dragon frantically bumped him with its head and the memory vanished. Alex reached out numb fingers to take hold of an armoured plate on its back.

Power tingled at his fingertips and flooded his bones with warmth. For his entire life he had feared the ocean.

Now he knew he belonged there. When his lungs demanded air, Alex *breathed*. Oxygen poured into his lungs instead of the frigid sting of salt water. A bubble of air girdled his mouth and nose like a breathing mask.

The Water Dragon streamed through the tunnel. Alex clung to its back and revelled in how the water seemed to part for them, opening a billowing channel of safe passage.

Seconds later they broke the surface and hands hauled him onto a slimy shelf of rock.

Zoey crouched over him, pawing at him like he might dissolve into sodden sand. She must have found the tunnel too.

"I lost you," she said. "I didn't know if you were ahead or behind me."

Anil watched anxiously while Bridget shook her brother by the shoulders hard enough to rattle his teeth.

"Can you breathe?" she said. "No *way* am I giving you mouth-to-mouth."

Alex dislodged her by breaking into a wet, wracking cough. The air bubble had burst and briny water dribbled from his lips. "I'm okay," he sputtered. "The Water Dragon saved me."

It was partly true. The dragon had rescued him from the tunnel by showing him he had the power to save himself. It had been Alex who created the bubble of precious breath.

Only the topmost layer of the rock shelf was left dry by the high tide. The Water Dragon floated alongside it, watching closely. It squeezed its eyes and lifted its head, a wistful lowing resonating in its throat. *An apology*, Alex felt. For the unjust revenge it had sought against Grandma and him. The memory had shown Alex the dragon's anguish at finding its egg stolen, the blind rage that had driven its vendetta. Now it had heard Callis's story and finally knew exactly who was responsible for the theft.

"Grandma still felt responsible," Alex told the Water Dragon. "She wanted to make it right."

Zoey stepped up behind him. "I think you finally did."

The Water Dragon sighed and turned over backwards to drift in the water. The cavern may only have been a larger cage, but the dragon seemed to relish the space. It knew this place, had sheltered here over centuries and more.

The tide was high enough that the cave entrance was nowhere to be seen.

"We'll have to wait for the tide to go out," said Anil.

"Those boats will be patrolling every inch of the bay," said Zoey. "If the Water Dragon tries to swim for it now they'll catch the heck out of it."

The chase had made it difficult to count exactly how many boats had been out there. But Callis wouldn't take any chances. Every boat would be equipped with nets and harpoons and sonar to search underwater. The bay would serve as a natural trap. The Water Dragon would only be safe if it reached the open ocean beyond.

"We'll have to find another way," said Alex.

Carefully, Bridget took a seat beside Alex and slung an arm around his shoulder. Zoey hunkered down eagerly on her other side, pressing close. They were all soaked and shivering, but huddling together quickly made him feel warm again.

"Can I get in there?" asked Anil.

"No," answered Zoey, shuffling closer to Alex. Then she caught herself, wincing apologetically, before moving aside so that Anil could join the huddle.

Although the water inside the cavern was as dirty as the bay outside, it was no longer full of whatever chemicals the Station had been pumping into it. As the dragon ducked and looped under the surface, Alex felt its strength returning in a trickle.

"Back at the jetty," said Zoey. "That power came from you, not the dragon, didn't it?"

Alex smiled shyly. "Yeah, that was me. I just breathed underwater too."

"I can't believe it! How long have you had *powers*?"

"Not long," said Alex. "I'm still working out how to use them."

"So they might get stronger? Maybe you'll turn into a fish person!"

Alex studied the palm of his hand as if the answer would be etched there. "Maybe." He glanced around at the others. "You were all amazing tonight."

Zoey scoffed. "We're hiding from the bad guy in a cave."

"Yeah, but we *did it*. We got the dragon out! Your drone worked perfectly."

Zoey smiled with pride.

"And you were so strong!" Alex continued, squeezing Bridget's arm. "Anil, that had to be a new record for holding your breath."

"I reckon so, yeah." Anil paused a moment as if he wasn't sure he should say anything more. "I'm really glad you let me be part of it."

Bridget hugged him hard enough that they heard his bones creak.

"We couldn't have done it without you, Tunnel Turtle," said Zoey.

After a while, Bridget's stomach began to rumble. The noise was loud enough to echo around the walls, like a monster growling deep inside the tunnels. The Water Dragon poked its head above the water to answer with a mournful rumble of its own.

"Oh, whatever," Bridget told it. "I need at least five

thousand calories a day just to, like, *maintain* my muscle mass."

Zoey sighed. "I'm starving."

Now that he had warmed up a little, Alex had to admit he was getting hungry too. It would be a long wait until morning and low tide.

The water stirred at the edge of the rock shelf. A furry brown head peeked above the surface. Droplets beaded on the sea otter's coat as it clambered onto the shore, gripping something in its mouth.

Anil peered closer. "Is that...?"

A chocolate bar was clenched between the otter's teeth. It hurried over to them and dropped the offering at Alex's feet.

"For us?" he asked.

"Obviously!" said Bridget, lunging for the chocolate.

The rest of the otters emerged from the water, carrying a banana, a packet of crisps, and a soggy egg-and-cress sandwich respectively.

Kraken rode on the last otter's back. When she spotted Alex she launched herself into his arms.

"It's good to see you too, Your Ladyship," said Alex.

The water was churning now. More sea creatures appeared with treats. Turtles carried packets of biscuits on their shells. A seal slapped onto the rock to drop a waterlogged box of cereal. Lobsters and crabs clicked ashore with doughnuts looped over their claws. Deeper in the water, otherworldly billowing shapes smouldered, jellyfish drifting into the cavern. Shoals of fish flashed silver as they revolved in tight balls.

A geyser of water erupted as a dolphin lifted its head to chirrup a greeting. A can of fizzy drink rolled from its mouth, an otter ferrying it to shore.

Deliveries made, the new arrivals gathered around the Water Dragon to nuzzle its enormous head and nose at its armoured sides, swimming closely around it like a shield.

"They must have sensed when the dragon returned to the ocean," said Alex.

"Amazing," said Anil through a mouthful of biscuits. Bridget seized the opening to snatch the packet from him and pour the rest into her mouth.

"It looks like an army," said Zoey, stepping up beside Alex. "You think you can command this many?"

Alex watched the assembly of animals and smiled. With the Water Dragon by his side, he felt like he could do anything.

CHAPTER TWENTY-THREE

THE SECOND SIEGE OF HAVEN BAY

A greasy otter rolling across Alex's face proved an effective wake-up call. When he rubbed the sleep from his eyes and sat up he found the others snuggled warmly around him.

Pale daylight lit the cavern. The tide had fallen back and the cavern entrance was open. The lower shelf of the rock was revealed, shining with a fresh helping of seaweed.

Alex scrambled upright to see where the Water Dragon had gone. The channel behind the rock platform was still full of seawater. The dragon was nestled safely inside, eyes closed and breathing gently.

Gradually, the others stirred awake. Zoey peeled Kraken off her face, while Bridget blearily lifted her head from the shell of the turtle she had employed as a pillow. Anil jumped to his feet, the crabs that had settled on him for the night tumbling off like flaking scales.

"It feels like I slept on a pile of rusty lawnmower blades," said Zoey, twisting her neck sideways with a sickening *crunch.*

Bridget prised a limpet from her left bicep. "Not *my* idea of glamping."

A human silhouette appeared in the mouth of the cavern. Grandpa picked his way across the stony sand to reach them.

"Rough night?" he said, stepping carefully up onto the rock.

Alex slipped and slid down to envelop him in a hug. "You're safe."

"They chased me for a good while, 'til they realized there weren't no dragon in my van. They sloped off back to their boats to wait it out," said Grandpa. "I made good and sure nobody followed me. Callis don't know you're 'ere."

Behind them, the Water Dragon lingered close to the rock, scaly snout snuffling at the air. The narrow channel inside the cavern was still pretty filthy, but Alex was sure the dragon already looked healthier. Bigger. The grey tinge of its scales had washed away to reveal sparkling greens and blues. Its eyes had cleared to piercing black pearls.

"It knows Grandma was innocent," Alex said.

Grandpa gasped and, after a moment to steel himself, stretched a hand towards the Water Dragon. It reared from the water to push its muzzle into the caress of his fingers. Grandpa laughed, face shining with delight.

The others made their way down the rock, the otters following to join the huddle.

"Callis isn't givin' up easy," said Grandpa. "His men are out in force this mornin'. The only way to get here unseen was from the far side of the bay."

"So we're trapped?" asked Zoey.

"The bay is sealed up tight. Callis's takin' a leaf right out of his ancestor's book. He's waitin' for the next high tide. If the dragon swims for it, they'll snap it up in a heartbeat. If not, they'll come searching."

Zoey turned to Alex. "Can't you just..." She swept her arms through the air and made a dramatic crashing sound. "Use your superpowers?"

Alex shook his head. "I'm not strong enough, and the dragon needs to recover from last night. But if we stay here Callis will find us."

Everybody – including the animals – fell quiet. Hundreds of years ago, the Water Dragon had summoned a storm to destroy Brineblood's blockade. If it was too weak to do that now, against much more advanced technology, they would have to find another way.

"We tell him we're giving up," said Alex.

Everybody whirled around to look at him. "*What?*"

"We're not *actually* giving up! If we pretend we're going to hand over the dragon out on the water, we can draw his boats away so there's a gap in the blockade. The Water Dragon can swim for it from here."

Grandpa didn't appear convinced. "He'll smell a rat."

"We need a bigger distraction," said Zoey, before breaking into a mischievous grin. "I've got a heck of an idea."

Bridget's face lit up. "Me too."

When they told him their plans, Alex couldn't help but smile too.

"Somebody has to stay here with the Water Dragon," he said.

Anil raised his hand. "I can do it."

"The rest of us will go out and meet Callis. As soon as we've lured the blockade away, we'll give a signal for you to send the dragon swimming for it."

"The flare gun!" exclaimed Zoey. "Oh, *please* let me use the flare gun I stole – I mean, *confiscated* – from Callis's ship."

Alex rubbed his fingers across the Water Dragon's scaly head. Energy sparked between them. The dragon blinked, white sheaths sliding across its eyes.

"You're getting stronger already," he whispered. "We're

going to get you out of here. I might not see you again, if everything goes to plan. Thank you for everything you've done for me."

The dragon rumbled deep in its throat. Alex turned away as tears stung his eyes. It had only been a few days, but his whole life had changed. An ancient power had been roused inside him and he was no longer scared of the ocean, separated from who he really was.

And that meant he was no longer scared of facing off against Callis one last time.

The others were gathering at the foot of the rock. He joined them and they set off towards the cavern entrance.

"Watch for the flare!" Alex called over his shoulder, voice bouncing around the rocky walls.

"We'll be ready!" Anil shouted back.

Bright morning light dazzled them. A thin layer of clouds was rapidly melting under the glow of the rising sun. Pink edged the sky and simmered on the peaceful surface of the bay. Seabirds detached from the cliff and hovered lazily overhead.

The blockade of boats appeared as a dotted line across the mouth of the bay. The narrow spaces between them bobbed with floats attached to nets hidden underwater. If anything tried to slip underneath it would be caught. More boats patrolled the water. Grandpa took them along a path that hugged the cliffs and led in the opposite direction from town to avoid being spotted.

"They're not going to give up, are they?" said Zoey quietly.

"No," replied Alex. "But neither are we."

At the far side of the bay the cliffs dropped low again to rejoin the surf. They followed the shoreline to a hidden stony beach. The ice cream van waited for them and they began the journey back to town by road.

"What happens when Callis clocks we don't have the Water Dragon with us at the handover?" asked Grandpa.

"It'll be a race. The dragon will have to reach the open ocean before any of the boats can stop it," said Alex. "That's why we need to keep Callis busy for as long as possible."

Although the Water Dragon's strength was returning, Alex didn't know if it had recovered enough to win such a chase. Callis had come so close to successfully capturing it. There was no way he would let it go without a fight.

When they reached town everybody jumped out of the van. Townspeople had gathered in groups along the sea wall to peer out at the patrolling boats.

"It's just one thing after another, these days," grumbled Mrs Bilge. "If I were younger I'd go out there and have a stern word."

"Someone should show them who's boss," agreed Mr Ballister.

The high street was busier than usual. Strangers were peering into shop windows and searching alleys between buildings. They had to be Callis's crew.

"I'll get them to deliver a message to Callis that we're willing to surrender. Can you meet me at the harbour in an hour?" asked Alex.

"Oh yes," said Zoey.

Bridget rolled her shoulders. "I wouldn't miss it."

Their eyes glowed with trouble. Alex couldn't wait for them to unleash what they each had planned.

"This is our last chance to save the dragon," he said. "Let's make it count."

CHAPTER TWENTY-FOUR

HECK BREAKS LOOSE

Two vessels were waiting when they returned to the harbour. The first was a long rowing boat, Grandpa seated at the prow. The other was a pedal boat shaped like a swan, long neck stretching forward with a rope wrapped around it like a scarf and its wings splayed gawkily to form the craft's sides.

"Best I could rustle up on short notice," said Grandpa.

Zoey and Mr Wu arrived, dragging a long package wrapped in a blanket between them. When Alex went to help, he found a fanned mermaid's tail poking out from the end.

"Nobody got to see my dad's model sea monster at the ceremony yesterday," said Zoey. "I think it deserves another chance."

"I told you art is useful," added Mr Wu.

Zoey stuck her tongue out at him and they both laughed.

Together they dragged the model sea monster into the rowing boat and laid it across the damp planks.

"If Callis takes a proper look, he'll see it's a decoy," said Alex. "He just needs to believe it's real for long enough to open up a gap in the blockade."

Footsteps tramped along the jetty towards them. Alex turned back to find Bridget leading a troop of figures wearing bulky raincoats, hoods hanging low enough to hide their faces.

"How did you convince them?" Alex asked his sister.

Bridget arched an eyebrow and smiled. "I told them there was a chance to use their strength for something that really matters."

The anonymous arrivals filed into the rowing boat, lining the benches on either side, the dragon decoy lying at their feet.

Alex turned to look across the bay. The blockade was a series of dark shapes barricading the open ocean beyond. A larger boat lingered ahead of the others, waiting impatiently for their arrival on the water.

"We live alongside our tiny slice of sea, and we haven't cared for it like we should," said Grandpa, standing on the jetty. "This same damage is bein' done all over the world.

The ocean is the most precious thing we have on this planet. If we keep it safe and well, it'll do the same for us." He turned to peer out towards the blockade. "Too many people care more about abusin' it to line their pockets."

Bridget took the last remaining spot in the rowing boat, while Alex and Zoey shared the seats on the swan.

"Ready for this?" Alex asked.

Zoey replied by pulling a black marker pen from her pocket and reaching forward to draw a set of angry eyebrows on the swan's face.

Alex raised his voice so the others would hear. "Callis is expecting us. Let's not keep him waiting!"

Grandpa and Mr Wu waved them off as they pushed away from the jetty. The hooded figures drew the oars powerfully through the water in perfect synchronicity. Alex and Zoey had to pump their legs hard to keep up.

Clouds had strayed across the sun and the ocean reflected their brooding grey. Around the swan boat, dolphins and seals matched their speed, crabs clinging to their backs as they swam through an honour guard of jellyfish. This sea-animal army sank away out of sight as they drew closer to the blockade.

Crew lined every deck, closely watching the slender spaces between boats, ready to raise the alarm and close up tight.

"Do you think we can pull this off?" whispered Alex.

Zoey shrugged. "So far our plans have been mostly rubbish, but they've also mostly worked."

The larger ship – the cage no doubt finished and waiting in its belly – peeled away from the rest and sped towards them, waves frothing behind it. A few others left the blockade to follow and surround them with their nets. Alex caught Bridget's eye. They exchanged a nod, bracing themselves for whatever happened next.

Alex turned his gaze across the bay towards the cliffs. Inside the cavern, Anil would be waiting for the signal. The distance from the cliffs to the mouth of the bay looked impossibly far from here.

Pedalling hard, Alex brought the swan ahead of the rowing boat to meet Callis's craft. The turbulence of its engine set the water chopping and slapping as it bore down on them. The other boats formed up on either side to enclose them in a tight semicircle.

Alex peered anxiously beyond them. There was a gap in the blockade now, the line of nets opened up, but nowhere near big enough that it couldn't be closed quickly to keep the Water Dragon from escaping.

The main boat loomed over them. Callis stepped out onto the deck. The harpoon gun, fully loaded, once again rested idly against his shoulder.

"Who are they?" he growled, nodding to the hooded figures seated inside the rowing boat.

"We needed help lifting it," Alex shouted back, thinking quickly.

Callis casually shifted the harpoon to his other shoulder. "Whatever tricks you've got up your sleeve, they won't work."

In reply, Alex simply pointed to the rowing boat. There was wriggling movement inside the blanket. The dragon decoy's tail glinted in the sun. Callis's eyes immediately turned steely with greed. He waved to the guards standing behind him.

"Go and fetch it! Quickly!"

The guards began to clamber down towards the rowing boat.

"You don't deserve the Water Dragon," shouted Alex.

Callis grinned lazily. "Nobody has been searching for it as long as me. I've *earned* it. I don't know how you've learned to *leech* its powers, but it won't last."

"Somebody sounds jealous," said Zoey.

The guards boarded the rowing boat, making it sink low in the water and rock precariously side to side as they surrounded the decoy.

"The world needs me to wield this power," growled Callis. "It's the only way to pull us back from the brink."

Alex shook his head. "You're only making sure that you get rich while the places that can't afford you get worse and worse."

One of the guards reached down to lift an edge of the blanket. From underneath it came an excited chattering, making the guard hesitate.

"Bring it aboard, I don't have all day!" Callis barked.

The guard whipped the blanket away. Exposed, the "dragon" was clearly a model cobbled together from junk, paint flaking away into the bottom of the boat. Four otters huddled alongside it.

Callis reared up in fury. "Where is it?"

The otters leaped at the guards, looking like fuzzy sausages flashing with teeth and claws.

Bridget stood at the head of the boat and raised a fist. "Time to issue tickets for the gun show!"

The hooded figures threw off their raincoats to reveal the weightlifting team dressed in skintight Lycra leotards. Their monstrous biceps flexed as they threw the guards over the sides and rushed to board Callis's boat. Bridget and Baron Barge waded into the fight side by side.

Alex turned to Zoey. "It's time."

Grinning, she pulled out the bright red flare gun she had taken from Callis's ship and lifted it above her head.

"I have a feeling I'm going to enjoy this."

The sharp *pop* of the launching flare was chased by the lingering *hiss* of it arcing into the sky above the boats. It paused at the top of its white smoke trail, as if it might simply fizzle to nothing, before bursting into a livid spray of pink fireworks. The percussive *bang* reached them a moment later.

"Get them!" bellowed Alex.

And all heck broke loose.

CHAPTER TWENTY-FIVE

THE SHARP END OF
THE HARPOON

A strutting horde of muscle squeezed into straining leotards swarmed the deck of Callis's boat, using their strength to help each other aboard. Guards rushed forward to meet them. The bodybuilders plucked them up effortlessly and hoisted them above their heads. One guard fell onto the deck for a throng of crabs to descend nipping upon him. Another was hurled overboard into a mass of jellyfish, the water fizzing as they bustled and stung. Flailing bodies hit the water like fleshy jetsam.

If they tried to climb back aboard, dolphins leaped from the waves to knock them away. The otters plunged into the water to cling to their hair and nip at their grasping fingers. Seabirds dive-bombed their heads.

Callis howled, backing away before the bodybuilders reached him.

"Do you think he's angry?" said Zoey with a grin as they watched from the swan boat.

"The angrier he gets the less attention he's paying."

Alex hoped Anil had seen the signal flare and would already have sent the Water Dragon out of the cavern. The commotion was luring more boats away from the blockade, leaving the mouth of the bay gaping open.

While Bridget's muscle-bound band fought across the deck, Alex unravelled the rope from around the swan's neck. A thick metal claw was attached to its end. Zoey took out her drone from the belly of the swan and hooked the rope around the doll's head.

"Now for some fancy flying," she said.

Her fingers flew across the controls as the drone launched. It skimmed over the churning surface of the water, dodging dolphins and swerving snapping turtles. Zoey sent it rushing towards the main propeller of Callis's boat. If they could tangle it up, there would be no way he could give chase.

At the last moment, Callis spotted the drone and swung the barrel of his harpoon gun. One shot smashed the drone out of the air and sent it spiralling into the waves. The rope detached and sank after it.

"You'll pay for that!" shouted Zoey.

Callis reloaded the gun, but the weightlifter marauders pushed him back before he could aim another shot. Kraken held herself tall on top of Alex's head and fired jets of water at guards emerging from below decks to join the skirmish. A seal charged across the deck and bowled them over. The seabirds wheeled away to focus on the other boats pulling into attack range.

Casting his eyes around, Callis finally recognized that he was losing the battle. He snarled fiercely and levelled his harpoon straight at the swan boat.

"Duck!" shouted Alex.

"I'm pretty sure it's a swan," replied Zoey.

Before Callis could pull the trigger, somebody barrelled into his shoulder from behind and knocked him off balance. It was Mayor Parch, tattered vestments streaming, hands cuffed behind his back.

"This is intolerable!" he howled. "I will not be held captive in such *disrespectful* conditions."

The blockade had completely broken apart now. Before he could stop himself, Alex glanced across the bay. A whirlwind of dark-winged birds – no, *bats!* – formed an aerial guard. Underneath them a billowing ripple raced through the ocean towards the mouth of the bay.

Callis followed Alex's gaze. His eyes grew wide as he

spotted the movement in the water. Growling, he hurried towards the front of the boat, shoving guards out of the way.

"No!" Alex shouted.

Bridget hurried back to haul Alex and Zoey onto the deck of Callis's boat, just as the engines roared and the boat lurched away. Everybody clung to the rail to keep from toppling overboard. The boat rapidly picked up speed as Callis dashed straight towards the Water Dragon.

"We have to stop him!" shouted Alex.

The boat was moving too quickly for anyone to do anything but hold on. Birds swooped at Callis's head but he ignored the swipes of their talons and snaps of their beaks.

Moments later the Water Dragon's escape party came into full view. The ocean foamed around the undulating flanks of the bolting dragon, its nimble body cresting the waves in rolling loops. Anil rode beside it on the back of a dolphin, shouting encouragement. Overhead, Pinch led a black and white squadron of gulls and bats.

Callis steered the boat to cut off the Water Dragon's path to the mouth of the bay.

"That's my dragon!" shouted Callis.

He cut the engine. The boat drifted directly in front of the dragon, bats billowing and shoals of fish streaming protectively around it.

"Go underneath!" Anil shouted.

All the dragon had to do was dive under the hull of the boat and swim for freedom. Instead it paused to lift its head above the waves, casting its eyes anxiously around until they settled on Alex.

"It's checking you're okay," said Zoey.

"Go!" Alex shouted. "The bay is open!"

But Callis had seen it too. He whirled around to point the harpoon directly at Alex.

"If it goes anywhere, I'll shoot."

Alex froze, raising his arms to hold the others behind him. The wicked point of the harpoon was aimed square at his chest. In the water, the dragon bellowed its fury but made no move to escape or attack.

"You won't take the dragon from me!" shouted Callis, spit flying from his mouth.

"It doesn't belong to you. It doesn't belong to anybody," said Alex.

Behind Callis, somebody staggered to their feet. It was Mayor Parch, hands still lashed behind his back.

"Forty years!" cried Callis. "I've always wanted to be like you! To wield the power of my ancestor! Instead I'm nothing more than a pathetic *human*, separated from the water! What makes you special?"

Alex tried to keep his eyes from the mayor creeping

closer. "The dragon trusted me. It *let me* use this power. Your whole life was spent on the ocean, but you only ever took from it instead of protecting it. If you really want to be like me, you'll let the dragon go free."

Slowly, Callis's eyes softened. He lowered his weapon. The mayor saw his opening and lunged forwards. Callis caught the movement in the corner of his vision and dodged aside, making Parch trip over his robes and fall in a heap.

When Callis turned his eyes back on Alex they had once again grown cold and hard.

"If I can't have it, nobody can!"

Callis swung around to aim the harpoon at the Water Dragon stalled in the surf below.

"Don't!" screamed Alex.

The gun fired with a rush of air and a sharp metallic *clang*. A brief fragment of quiet tracked its flight through the air, the only sound the thin whistling song of the trailing cable.

Then the harpoon pierced the flesh of the Water Dragon's side with a terrible *thud*.

CHAPTER TWENTY-SIX

THE OCEAN SINGS
ITS WRATH

The dragon arched out of the water in a roar of pain and fury. Its tremorous howl sent the bats and seabirds scattering.

A long cable pulled tight between the harpoon embedded in the Water Dragon's side and the gun still in Callis's grip. Mouth gaping, the dragon thrashed its armoured sides, fighting to pull free. Callis fitted the gun into a cradle attached to the boat and locked it firmly into place.

Alex ran towards him. "You don't know what you've done!"

A manic grin sliced across the poacher's face. "I've finally caught it! I'm the master of the ocean now!"

The Water Dragon howled, rolling sideways, the cable only clinging tighter. Dark blood clouded the churning water as it poured from the wound. Anil urged his dolphin closer. It nosed at where the harpoon had bitten deep and keened with sorrow.

"Should I try and pull it out?" asked Anil.

"Leave it!" Zoey shouted back. "The more it struggles, the worse it gets!"

Helpless, Anil was forced to retreat as the dragon thrashed against the pull of the cable.

Alex turned to Callis. "You have to let it go."

Callis ignored him and pressed a button. The cable began to reel up, towing the dragon closer. The front of the boat split apart, opening up to where the cage was ready and waiting.

Alex took the opportunity to pounce. He caught Callis off balance and sent them both lumbering across the deck. Bridget and the bodybuilders joined him, pinning Callis down under their weight.

"It's too late!" he cackled.

The heartbreaking cries of the Water Dragon rent the air. The noise pulsed through the water, as if it were wrenching the invisible threads under the ocean to resound around the entire planet. Alex refused to let it be a death knell.

The others held Callis while Alex ran across the deck. He tried to release the harpoon gun but it was locked tight in its cradle.

"Did you really think you could win?" mocked Callis.

"I have to try!" said Alex.

Callis barked a taunting laugh. "Why?"

"Because even when it looks like everything is stacked against you, even when you're more scared than you've ever been, you still have to fight for what you believe is right."

Below, the Water Dragon stopped thrashing to lift its head above the blood-frothed waves. Its pearlescent eyes met Alex's for the briefest moment before they turned white. The membrane around its neck inflated, round and buoyant, holding it high in the water. A green glow spread across its scales, brighter than Alex had ever seen. An aurora of energy surged from its body and pulsed across the surface of the bay.

The triumphant smile dropped from Callis's face. "It can't have regained its powers yet."

Alex closed his eyes and heard the ocean singing an ancient hymn. Energy seemed to return in ripples across the bay, as if every living thing under the waves was answering the dragon's call, lending a little of its life force.

Callis tried to struggle free but Bridget and the bodybuilders easily held him helpless.

Tendrils of ocean curled around the harpoon and wrested it loose, exposing the deep wound in the Water Dragon's side. The bloodstained metal barb sank into the waves and the cable fell harmlessly slack.

All around the boat the water began to seethe and swell. Waves rose up like living creatures, foamy edges reaching for the sky before they came crashing back down. They mingled and fused, swirling around each other in a primal dance. Higher they rose, and higher, until they twisted together into a spinning pillar of water that loomed high above the boat.

The sky descended. Clouds dipped low to catch the raging pillar and hoist it aloft. The sea animals scattered, taking Anil with them, the birds hurrying out of range. The Water Dragon growled like a thousand peals of thunder.

Slowly, the furious monolith of water began to move towards them.

Zoey grabbed Alex's shoulder. "It knows we're on its side, right?"

Alex closed his eyes and listened to the song of the ocean. Under the maddened din of the rushing vortex, he felt the ripples of energy nudge against him. The power was being channelled by the Water Dragon, but hadn't it shown him how to use it too? The dragon wouldn't hurt them because it knew Alex wouldn't let that happen.

The waterspout hit the boat. Everybody clung desperately to the rail as they were snatched high into the air, spiralling viciously upwards, spray whipping at their faces and tearing their clothes. The boat groaned and creaked. Boards and boxes broke off and flew away in the force of the storm.

"We have to jump!" shouted Alex over the deafening noise.

Zoey gaped at him. "You can't be serious!"

Although it was hard to see through the whirling walls of the waterspout, they knew it was a long drop to the sea below.

Alex held out his hand. "Trust me."

Zoey took his hand. The other she offered to Bridget, who in turn reached for Baron. Soon they had formed a human chain along the deck of the boat, Mayor Parch forming its end.

"What about him?" said Zoey.

Free of the bodybuilders, Callis clung to the railing as the deck jolted and cracked underneath him. The poacher deserved to be left behind. He had taken so much from the ocean. Didn't it deserve to take him in return? The world would be safer without him.

Except Alex knew he couldn't just leave the man to his fate.

"Come with us!" Alex shouted, extending his free hand.

Callis gazed back at him doubtfully, before reaching to take it.

Too late. The deck splintered, splitting apart and stranding Callis out of reach.

"Keep your powers hidden," the defeated poacher shouted. "There will be others who will try to take them."

The boards of the deck peeled away like sticking plasters in the force of the wind. The windows of the cockpit blew out and the metal railings began to buckle. Callis fell away out of sight. In moments, the whole boat would be in pieces.

Together, the group faced the ferocious deluge of the waterspout.

"Jump!" Alex shouted.

The wind plucked them instantly into the air. Their bodies sprawled through a blustering wall of water. Still, Alex held tight to Zoey's hand as they were ousted from the waterspout and the fuming ocean rose up to meet them.

Alex hit the water hard. The chain of hands broke apart. Darkness closed over his head. The height of the fall had pushed him deep beneath the waves. For a moment he expected the ache of familiar panic inside his chest. When it didn't come, he instead reached out to grasp a thread of the ocean.

A bubble of oxygen closed around his nose and mouth. He took a deep breath of precious air and turned in the water.

Zoey and Bridget were kicking their way through the tumult to try and reach the surface. Alex waved a hand to make oxygen bubbles inflate over their faces too. The bodybuilders received them next, the air helping to lift their unwieldy limbs through the water. Lastly, he sent a bubble to Mayor Parch, robes billowing around him like a cloak of seaweed.

By the time they burst through the roiling surface of the bay together the waterspout had moved away. Scraps of wood and metal splashed down around them, the vortex spitting out the bones of the boat. There was no sign of Raze Callis at all.

The spout lurched across the bay, heading straight for the Station on the far side of the curving coast. It smashed into the concrete building with irresistible force. The raging water tore through the middle of the building, chewing it into pieces.

Only when the Station was reduced to crumbs did the storm lose its power. The sky released the top of the pillar and it faltered, sinking into the waves like a scuppered ship. The bay swallowed it, rugged surf returning to its familiar tranquil rhythm.

Nearby, the glow of the Water Dragon dwindled. The bleeding creature sagged in the water, the threads of power falling slack.

CHAPTER TWENTY-SEVEN

AFTER THE STORM

Alex swam across the bay and reached the Water Dragon as it listed sideways in the newly stilled waves.

"You did it," he said. "You can go free."

The blockade of boats had been scattered around the bay like toys. There was nothing to prevent the dragon's escape. But every scrap of its energy had been spent on conjuring the storm, and the wound in its flank drained it further.

The dragon lifted its regal head and blinked wearily.

"I knew the ocean was powerful. I was frightened of it for so long," Alex said. "You showed me that it's a part of who I am. Of who we all are."

He hugged the creature's neck tightly, as if he could

squeeze life through the scales rough against his skin. The Water Dragon rolled sideways, curling into a helix, struggling to keep itself afloat.

"You can't die," wept Alex. "We need you."

Around him, the water grew agitated again. But it was not the storm rekindling. Sea animals shoved Alex aside to gather around the wounded dragon. The otters climbed over its side and tenderly used their claws to prise open the coils its body had constricted into. Once the length of its body was exposed, dolphins wedged themselves on either side of the dragon like floats on a barge, lifting it from the middle. Seals hefted its head above the waves, while a shimmering shoal of fish teemed around its tail. Together they formed a living life raft to hold the Water Dragon afloat.

Something plopped onto Alex's head. Octopus arms trailed over his face.

"You need to go too?" he said.

Kraken jumped across to land on the Water Dragon's neck and lifted a front arm to give him a flailing wave.

"Bye, octopus buddy," Zoey said, swimming up beside him.

Alex reached out a hand and placed it gently on the dragon's snout. It nuzzled his fingers weakly, scales hard against his palm.

"I'll miss you," he said.

Anil slipped off the back of his dolphin so it could join the other animals. The living raft began to move, carrying the Water Dragon away from them towards the open mouth of the bay.

"Do you think it'll be okay?" asked Anil.

The deep sadness in his belly couldn't keep a smile from spreading across Alex's face. "The dragon heals the ocean. The ocean will heal it in return."

The flotilla of animals reached the mouth of the bay. The clouds parted overhead, pouring dazzling sunshine over the waves.

Something bumped into Alex's back. He turned to find the swan boat, missing its beak and most of its white paint stripped away. Grandpa sat behind the pedals. He reached down to squeeze Alex's shoulder.

"Yer grandma would be so proud of you."

Alex smiled up at him. "She would be proud of all of us."

Scraps of wood and metal still floated on the gently lapping waves in the aftermath of the storm. Still, the sun delved deep into the water, reaching the rocks and seaweed of the seabed far below them. The oil and filth had evaporated.

"The dragon cleaned the bay," said Zoey.

Alex peered out towards the open ocean. The raft of animals was almost out of sight. Framed between the wide-set edges of the curving coast, they watched the Water Dragon slip away to sea and safety.

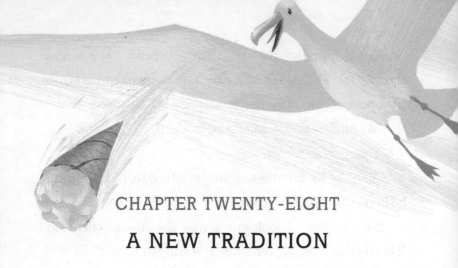

CHAPTER TWENTY-EIGHT

A NEW TRADITION

One month later

Spectators packed the beach, waving banners and snapping photographs on their phones, waiting for the ceremony to begin. Although most of the locals had turned out – Mrs Bilge heaved Cannonball above her head for a better view while Mr Ballister patrolled the sands with an ice cream cone in each hand – plenty of tourists were also in attendance. Word had quickly spread that Haven Bay was clean again. Grandpa's ice cream van had a queue as long as the sea wall.

"Are you ready for this?" asked Zoey.

Alex gulped. "I think so."

They stood at the edge of the water, cool tide lapping around their bare feet. A small, circular raft built from driftwood bobbed on the waves behind them. Zoey signalled for Bridget to lower the box she had carried from the boatyard.

"Want me to open it?" asked Bridget.

"Hang on a second."

"*Some* of us are missing weightlifting team training to be here," Bridget grumbled.

Zoey turned to look out across the sun-dappled bay. "Do you think the Water Dragon is still out there?"

There had been no sign of the dragon since it had been taken injured out to sea. Still, Alex knew it was out there somewhere, recovering its strength. It was free again, and Alex felt that same yearning for freedom urge him towards the waves.

"It will come back," he said. "When it's ready."

In the last month, they had worked hard to make sure that from now on Haven Bay would always live up to its name. The town had voted unanimously to kick Mayor Parch out of office and pass laws to protect the water. No more mysterious facilities would be built. Instead, the aquarium on the hill had been demolished, and construction had begun on a wind farm to provide clean energy to the town and beyond.

Alex turned back to face the restless crowd. "Where's Anil? We can't start this without him."

They had rescued the Water Dragon together, so it only felt right that they remain a team to continue doing everything in their power to protect the bay.

Anil had been grounded for the entire month after the rescue. But now he stood with his mum, dad and an older boy that could only be his brother. They ruffled his hair proudly before ushering him towards his friends. Anil jogged over, covering his head against a slightly chewed falafel that fell from the sky.

"All of them took the day off specially to be here." Anil beamed. "They want to meet my new friends."

Zoey winced. "Are they still annoyed about the whole lying-to-them-and-putting-yourself-in-mortal-danger thing?"

"Only a little bit."

Alex cleared his throat to try and get the crowd's attention. "Thank you for joining me here today," he said, but they were too busy talking among themselves or enjoying the blazing sunshine.

"LISTEN UP, YOU MAGGOTS!" bellowed Zoey.

Everybody fell quiet and focused their attention squarely on the group at the front of the beach.

"You are here to help mark a new beginning for Haven Bay," Alex continued. "For centuries we held a tradition that remembered a man – a *monster* – who tried to bring these seas under his control. It's time for that ceremony to end – even if it means my dad will never have a chance to win best scarecrow."

At the front of the crowd, Dad wiped a single tear from his eye.

"It's time for a new tradition!" Alex continued. "A ceremony that will make us face up to the damage we have done to the ocean and recognize that we must keep doing more to protect it."

Behind him, a dolphin leaped from the water in a shimmering arc, before splashing back into the tide. A seal nipped playfully at its tail. The otters gathered on the sand and shook their fur to spray the crowd with water.

So many animals had come to live in Haven Bay now it was clean again. Alex would do whatever it took to keep them safe.

"Today, we celebrate the Water Dragon, and everything it does for us despite what we take from it."

Zoey signalled for Bridget to open the box and lift out its contents. Inside was an egg of turquoise sea glass, polished smooth by the ocean's rhythm, set inside a fitting of driftwood. Built into the egg was a sensor that would monitor pollution levels in the water. Zoey and her dad had worked together for almost the whole month to combine their skills and create something undeniably beautiful, undoubtedly useful, and altogether unlikely to catch fire or explode.

Mr and Mrs Wu watched from the front of the crowd, beaming with pride.

"Together," said Alex.

The four of them – Alex, Zoey, Bridget and Anil – gathered around the egg and lifted it. The rescue hadn't just awakened a deep connection between Alex and the dragon – it had forged a bond between the whole group that he was sure could never be broken.

They placed the egg inside its driftwood raft and turned to face the crowd.

"We can never truly return what was taken and lost," announced Alex. "This is not just a symbol of our regret. It's a promise that things will change."

From the serving window of the ice cream van, Grandpa smiled proudly and nodded for him to go.

Alex backed into the water and took up a rope of knotted seaweed tied to the raft. After securing it around his shoulders, he kicked off into the waves, towing the egg away from the beach. The crowd cheered and waved their banners behind him.

The water sparkled around Alex, cool and crisp against his skin. Strength flowed through him and he surged towards the mouth of the bay. The threads of the ocean, connected to everything in its domain, thrummed around him. The Water Dragon would be at the end of one of them, waiting for the right time to return.

Dolphins easily matched his speed, fins cutting through the surf. The otters rode on their backs like aquatic cowboys. Seals and rays and fish darted around him like overexcited children.

A few more strokes brought Alex to the mouth of the bay. The egg floated alongside him. He stopped for a moment to face the open ocean. The water glistened invitingly in the sunshine. The waves whispered reassurance.

For so many years he had avoided the water. Now Alex whooped for joy, kicked forwards, and swam safely out of the bay.

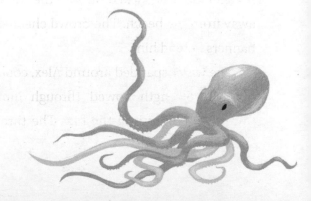

THERE ARE MORE OCEAN-SIZED ADVENTURES TO COME IN

ALEX NEPTUNE
⬦—◄ PIRATE HUNTER ►—⬦

When Haven Bay is attacked by pirates in a ship made of rubbish called *The Flying Dustman*, Alex realizes they are hunting for the water dragon's missing egg. So, he, Zoey and Anil set out to stop the pirates stealing its power, on a treasure hunt that takes them to a secret shipwreck where they must face three monstrous challenges.

READ ON FOR A SNEAK PEEK...

The threads of the ocean crowded around Alex, nipping at his skin as if daring him to play with them. He released one of the probes Zoey had invented to monitor the surrounding coastline and it floated in front of him. This close to shore it would drift back to the beach within minutes. Alex needed to summon a wave big enough to drag the probe out of the bay.

He spread his hands in the water and closed his eyes. Pictured a deep well of power inside himself. All he needed was to draw more of it to the surface. Hands clapped onto his shoulders, Zoey and Anil lending their support. It wasn't quite the same as his link to the Water Dragon, but it was close. The dragon hadn't given him power. It gave him access to what was already there.

Alex reached for a thread. A thunderous splashing sound made him think he had succeeded. He opened his eyes, expecting to find a towering wave standing at his command. Instead he saw a tremendously round seal barrelling towards him like a runaway boulder.

"No!" he shouted.

The seal knocked Alex off his feet, dunking him under the water. A wave washed them all to shore, Alex coughing and spluttering as the seal licked furiously at his face.

"Loaf!" shouted Zoey. "Get down!"

The seal was one of the first animals to make Haven Bay

its home after the water was safe again. A thickly spotted grey back faded to splodgy white over a colossal belly that made the animal almost as wide as he was long.

Zoey, Anil and the otters wrestled with Loaf until he used his stocky flippers to roll off Alex. Stumbling to his feet, Alex opened his mouth to scold the seal. Loaf peered up at him with wide, glistening eyes and twitched his whiskers. He was like an over-excited dog, always ready to play.

"I can't stay angry at that face," said Alex.

Loaf gave a yelping bark and coughed up a fish skeleton onto his feet.

The probe had survived the encounter intact and this time they let Anil swim it out to deeper water. It was almost dark by the time they finished, the sky growing an ever-inkier blue.

"Let's get these things working so I can make it home before my curfew," said Anil.

Zoey produced a laptop from her waterproof bag and began tapping away at a series of complicated menus onscreen. "They've reached the natural currents now," she said. "Time to fire them the heck up!"

With a flourish, she lifted a single finger high before bringing it down on the keyboard. A steady beeping fuzzed from the speakers.

"The probes check for changes in water quality and

temperature. They'll also alert us to any unexpected arrivals. You know, like maniacal poachers commanding a whole fleet of bad guys, that sort of thing."

"At least Callis is gone." Alex gazed out across the bay. Maybe the poacher's final act was to lie to him, make Alex believe there would be others after him so he would never feel safe. Maybe there was nothing bad out there at all.

The beeping from the laptop became more urgent. Zoey frowned at the screen. Alex felt a heavy anchor sink in the pit of his stomach.

"Is it going to explode?" asked Anil, backing away.

"My inventions don't do that any more! One of the probes is picking up a strange reading."

"Fun strange or bad strange?" asked Alex.

Zoey glared at the screen as if it was lying to her and began jabbing keys. "The probe says there's a big ship approaching the bay at speed. Apparently it's made from metal, wood and...crisp packets?"

Alex relaxed a little. "It must be broken."

"Maybe..." Zoey sagged before instantly perking up again. "Wait, another probe is giving the same reading! Tins, plastic bags, glass bottles...this ship is made from more materials than I can count!"

Frenzied splashing from the waterline made them all look up from the laptop. A girl was stumbling onto the beach, sodden clothes plastered to her skin, long strands of green hair sticking to her face. She staggered across the sand towards them, weaving dizzily side-to-side. Loaf and the otters moved in front of Alex to form a protective barrier.

"Are you okay?" he asked. She might have been a tourist who had swum out a little too far and struggled to make it back, except that she was fully dressed in mismatched shabby clothes, including tattered shoes that squelched as she walked.

"You're Alex Neptune," the girl said, short of breath, voice pinched by urgency. "You have to run."

A distant boom rolled across the water behind her. In the fading light, a ship was sailing into the mouth of the bay. Smoke drifted from its side. Snapping in the wind above its tall sails was a black flag, emblazoned with a white symbol Alex didn't know existed in real life.

The skull and crossbones.

Nobody realized the noise they had heard was a cannon firing until the first shot hit the town.

Find out what happens next in

Coming 2023

ACKNOWLEDGEMENTS

Ever since I wanted to be a writer, I've wanted to write a children's book. To do so with Usborne is a dream come true. It couldn't have happened without the support of a lot of people.

Massive thanks to the Usborne team, particularly my editor Sarah Stewart, who is such a champion of my writing, inexplicably laughs at my jokes, and appreciates the magic of Nicolas Cage. Thank you also to Anne and Hannah who helped whip *Alex Neptune* into shape.

My agent Ella Kahn has suffered alongside me through a few near misses with children's books, yet she never lost faith and always encouraged me to keep trying. This book would never have got over the line without her.

I'm usually incredibly secretive with my writing and keep drafts to myself for as long as possible. For *Alex Neptune*, I sought help from a number of close friends, who all deserve thanks.

Sarah, who encouraged me to embrace my weird ideas, and made me believe that what I had was worth persevering with. I couldn't have asked for better support in the long process of getting this book out into the world.

Non, who offered excellent, insightful feedback, guidance, and patience. There's nobody better to have in your corner.

Darran, my octopus oracle who never once minded when I messaged him at some random hour with a question about miscellaneous sea creatures.

Thank you also to Maisie and Leila for being invaluable sensitivity readers.

Lastly, I'd like to thank everybody who has supported my books so far. I hope a few of you will have joined me while I embark on something a little different.

**NO WATER SAUSAGES WERE
HARMED IN THE WRITING
OF THIS ADVENTURE.**

ABOUT THE AUTHOR

Having worked as a freelance games journalist and taught on a BA Creative Writing course for three years, David Owen's debut novel, *Panther*, was longlisted for the Carnegie Medal, and was followed by three further highly acclaimed YA novels. *Alex Neptune* is his first series for younger readers, born of his love for nail-biting heists, fantastical monsters and heartfelt friendships.